The

Mid*Wife*

Crisis

by

Lyndsey Gallagher

Following labour you meet the love of you're life... But who could predict the fate of the midwife?

DEDICATION

This book is dedicated to all the real life superheroes out there, the mothers, the should have been mothers, the want to be mothers, and those without mothers.

ACKNOWLEDGEMENTS

Thank you to my brilliant new editor Holly at Spotlight Editing. It's been a pleasure working with you.

A massive thank you to each and every single one of you who bought my debut novel and encouraged me to write another.

Last but not least, thank you to my amazing husband, my absolute rock. You are my Happily Ever After.

Contents

PROLGUE 2005

For some women, midwifery is a calling, born into their genes, a vocation, a purpose embedded inside their very core for as long as they can remember. The desire to aid new life, to witness a miracle, to be a part of something so much bigger than themselves. Evolution, procreation, the miracle of life.

Not me though, I accidently stumbled into it one Friday afternoon, a mere eighteen years of age when I was left with no choice but to deliver my neighbours sixth child alone, on the cold tiles of my mother's hallway.

'Please, Orla, you have to help me!' The front door flew open alarmingly, thudding hard against the plaster of the wall, rattling my brother's graduation photo hanging proudly at eye level for any passing caller to see. Naturally the door was unlocked, nobody ever locked their doors in Kinvarra, our picturesque coastal village on the east side of Galway.

We were a small community, everybody knew everything about everyone, the way it had always been. Sometimes this was a blessing but more often than not it was a nuisance. Like that one time I'd tried to sneak onto the night bus to the city aged fifteen. I was bound for an under eighteen's disco, looking older than my years in borrowed wet-look leggings and a sparkly halter neck top, only to be stopped in my tracks by my mother's, cousin's, husband who knew there was absolutely no chance I would be allowed to go to the city once it was dark. Not at that age anyway. To my utter disdain I was frog marched back to the house and grounded for the weekend for my boldness.

Kinvarra was beautiful, there was no doubt about it, tourists flocked by the bus load throughout the summer months to visit the quaint little cafés, browse in our traditionalsouvenir shops and leisurely gaze at the pier from one of the four restaurants lining the main street. It was scenic but sleepy and I was beginning to feel a little claustrophobic. The soles of my size five feet were decidedly itchy.

After finishing my Leaving Cert the previous summer, I'd taken a year off to work in my auntie's café whilst I struggled to plan what I should do with my life. There had been no point trying to apply for college because I had no idea which direction I wanted to go in. Until that day, when it became clearer than a tropical ocean on the sunniest of days.

Mrs Murphy lived in bungalow three houses down from ours, on the same side of the narrow country road that led to the beach. I babysat her children from time to time, all boys. They were a handful, full of energy and not fond of doing as they were told. But they were mighty craic, rolling, wrestling and fighting. When they began to tire, they used to snuggle into my arms to watch cartoons.

Mary was a no nonsense, strong, hard faced woman. She had to be to referee the five a side football team she'd created. But when her face broke into a crooked smile, you were left with no doubt that she had an absolute heart of gold. She would do anything for those boys.

'What is it? Are you okay?' I discarded the Harry Potter book I had been reading immediately, alarmed at the desperation in Mary Murphy's tone. It wasn't the done thing in the country to be openly emotional, most were too proud to outright ask for help. Many of the older generation would chew off their right arm before admitting they had a problem. It was bred into them, an old school type of unnecessary pride, ridiculous really because in a small community like ours almost anybody would do anything for their neighbour. In fact, if you took the time to trace back the village ancestry, it would likely reveal that most of us were distantly related in one way or another.

'It's the baby.' She clutched desperately at her enormous belly, panic obvious in her eyes, mirrored in my own widening stare as the full extent of the situation dawned on me. We were forty five minutes from the nearest hospital and as she howled in agony with the next onslaught of crippling contractions, I realised we'd be lucky if we managed to get as far as our local doctors surgery three miles away.

'Is your mother here?' She searched behind me hopefully, her eyes scanning the house for a more suitable adult. I only wished there was one -Mammy was at work.

'No, it's just me. Tell me what you need.' I ran to her and put my hand on her back, terrified as she doubled over in front of me. She clung to the wall for support, consumed by the relentless agony of the imminent birth of her sixth child.

I was in no way, shape or form equipped to deal with this situation, but she was better here with me than at home with the boys. It was in times like this,it became more obvious you lived in the countryside as we were miles away from the help she needed with no way to get there.

'Ring Malc please. He's at the store. It just came on so quickly, I didn't expect…' She fell forward landing on all fours as her body was enveloped by the next wave of excruciating contractions. I knew absolutely nothing about child birth. In fact, I'd only recently learnt the truth about the reproductive system, something I'd mostly taught myself as our awkward six foot four GAA fanatic of a biology teacher was surprisingly even more embarrassed saying words like 'vagina' than we were. But I'd watched enough television to know that those rapid contractions meant one thing and one thing only. That baby was coming, and soon.

I fumbled around in my jacket pocket desperately trying to locate my tiny red mobile phone, a Motorola that had been given to me as an eighteenth birthday present. I ran to the big bay window at the front of the house in an attempt to pick up enough of a signal to make the necessary calls. Looking up to where Mammy had positioned a statue of the Virgin Mary on the mantelpiece, next to her polished silver antique clock, I sent up the quickest prayer to the Virgin Mother herself to send help and quickly. For my sake - never mind Mary Murphy!

Sure, I was only a child myself, with no idea what the hell to do. Perspiration visible underneath my arms, I fought the rising panic in my chest with a deep gulp of air. As terrified as Mrs

Murphy was, I think I was worse. Trembling fingers struggled to dial the correct digits for the ambulance service. I described my current predicament and gave our address. The operator advised the estimated time of arrival was thirty two minutes. I wasn't even sure we had two minutes, let alone thirty two. How would I know? A low roar echoed through the old Georgian house from the hallway and I willed her with all my might to hang on.

Next I punched in the number for our local Centra where Malcolm was the manager; the call was answered on the second ring.

'Centra Kinvarra, Keira speaking how may I help you?' Keira Callen had been in my class at school, I used to fancy her older brother Kevin something rotten but he left for college three years earlier, never to be seen since. Rumour had it he'd got an internship in a fancy computer company in the States but you never know what to believe fourth hand in Kinvarra. It was equally as likely that he was working at a checkout in a Dublin petrol station, we'd never know either way. Both options seemed an exotic alternative to this sleepy town.

'Send Malcolm to my house quickly, Mary Murphy is in labour. I don't even know if he'll make it, she's close.' I gushed as fast as could, hanging up to call my mother on the off chance she may be somewhere in the vicinity. She worked for the HSE as a home help so she could be anywhere this side of the county. The answerphone cut in immediately, my luck was all out. Throwing the phone down onto the old fabric sofa in frustration, I accepted the stark fact that it was just Mary and I. Reluctantly, I returned to the tiled hallway where Mary appeared to be in her own world, rocking back and forth in a trancelike state.

Her enormous floral knickers were discarded on the floor inside the doorway, a sight I never dreamed I'd see, nor ever wanted to see again. Her past season summer dress carelessly hitched up around her enormous waist in anticipation. The baby was close. Mary should know, it wasn't like it was her first time. I'd heard it gets quicker with each child but Jesus, Mary and feckin' Joseph, how could she let it get this far? How could she do this to me?

Running up to the hot press, two stairs at a time I pulled down four huge bath towels and grabbed a bottle of water from the kitchen as I passed back through, trying to think of something useful to do.

'What do you need? Tell me.' I urged her as I crouched on the floor next to her and took her hand.

'I need a knife.' She panted for a couple of seconds before holding in a lung full of air and then blowing it out vigorously.

'A knife?' I moved to stand but her grip tightened on my right hand, her nails piercing my skin, intensifying the squeeze as the next contraction engulfed her.

'So I can cut Malcolm's balls off when he arrives.' She blew out another long, laboured burst of air. 'Slowly!' she screamed.

I tried not to erupt with laughter, though there was certainly nothing funny about our current predicament, nerves appeared to be getting the better of me.I'd almost sworn she was laughing herself, if it weren't for the sweat pouring from her brow and the tears of sheer agony rolling down her face. She clenched her teeth, suffering the next relentless onslaught.

If I'd ever considered having a baby, which thankfully I hadn't so far, this scenario would surely have put me off for life. Probably a good thing in some respects, I'd only been going out with my boyfriend for a few short months, although the whole town had us pegged for 'the next big day out.'

I watched as Mary leaned onto her elbows, freeing her hands to hitch her dress up further, feeling herself down there to check for a sign of the baby's head. I really didn't want to look, terrified and completely unprepared for what I would undoubtedly see, but in her perilous state she begged me to check for the baby. I couldn't refuse.

I saw parts of Mary that dayI never imagined I'd see of any woman. I shared in one of the most private, intimate experiences anyone could be part of in this unpredictable life. It was terrifying, bloody, shocking and animalistic. In those few moments, I realised with an unnerving clarity what it was to be a woman. I saw a real life super hero in the flesh with my very own young impressionable eyes. It was awe inspiring and it would change me forever.

Taking in an enormous breath, Mary let out an almighty roar of agony as she pushed out her sixth child, a fine sized beautiful baby girl with a head full of curly black hair.A tiny piercing shriek cut through the air, alarming me for a split second before I experienced a staggering rush of pure, incomprehensible emotion.

In those thirteen minutes of my life, I learned more than I had in my entire fourteen years in a classroom, enlightened by the overwhelming miracle of life. I'd witnessed first-hand what it was all about, human nature, evolution, survival.

Instantly Mary rolled onto her backside, the agony of those earlier seconds a distant memory already. She inspected the child briefly but thoroughly and wrapped her lovingly in one of the soft cream towels. She kissed her blissfully on the head, unmistakably enamoured with her. Laughing out loud in delight, she cradled her precious, healthy baby girl.

Tears flowed shamelessly from my eyes, drops of crystal clear enlightenment. It was the most beautiful, raw, worldly experience I'd witnessed in my whole short life. The way in which Mary looked down at that child you'd swear she was her first.Pure and utter adoration, a love like I'd never seen before. As I threw my arms around the two of them, no concern for the mess or blood, I found my calling in life. Or rather it found me.

CHAPTER ONE

—

Friday 6ᵗʰ November 2015

Edinburgh had been the place I'd called home for almost ten years, the city in which I'd studied and the place in which I'd chosen to stay. With its gothic architecture, rich history and extensive culture it was everything I'd grown to love since leaving Galway. There was always something going on, so much to see and do, after all that time I wasn't ready to leave. The endless choice of restaurants, bars, shops and entertainment appealed to me like nothing else.

Each August the city hosted the annual Fringe Festival and for the month of December, the ice rink and the big wheel took centre place in Princes Street Gardens along with the Christmas markets. I had settled here, content in my work and I'd made the best of friends. After qualifying as a midwife six years ago, I'd been lucky enough to have bagged myself a permanent contract in St Margaret's, the hospital that I'd done most of my placements in, much to Mammy's despair.

'When are you coming home?' She wailed down the phone at me as I broke the news to her.

'Ah, I will Mammy, I will. I'm just not ready yet. I want to get a bit more experience.' I told her unconvincingly.

'Can you not get experience in a hospital here?' She sighed reluctantly, but she was nevertheless delighted for me, proud as punch in a manner that only a mother could be.

We were a small family but very close. There was really only Mammy and my brother Jack. Daddy had left a long time ago, although it was almost unheard of at the time. Divorce wasn't actually legal in Ireland until 1997. Mammy never talked about it although she'd been burned very badly. I was small at the time, barely three years of age. Growing up I'd been the odd one out from a 'broken family'. I spent the early years of my childhood pining for Daddy, watching other girl's fathers doting on them, but Mammy more than made up for his absence in the end. I barely thought about him anymore. We had a huge amount of extended relations, aunts, uncles and cousins whose regular visits ensured we were never lonesome for long.

After years of shift work and a 'help to buy scheme' I'd managed to buy a reasonable sized two bedroom apartment at the top of Lothian Road. Signing the paperwork only three months ago, I was a home owner! Renting was dead money and much to my mother's horror, I wasn't ready to return to the Wild West just yet. I justified it as an investment, property prices were on the increase again following the years of recession. The truth was, I had no intention of going anywhere anytime soon. I'd made a great life, the best of friends and the security of a permanent position on the Labour Ward in St. Margaret's.

I hadn't found love since I arrived in the city, but I hadn't been looking for it either. A few had come and gone, none lasting more than a few weeks, nobody held any real interest for me. Online dating didn't appeal to me, nor talking to drunken strangers in bars, so unless my personal Prince Charming arrived at the Labour Ward, there was probably zero chance of me running into him. I was happy with things the way they were, not everybody needed or wanted the Happily Ever After. Life was perfect the way it was. Besides, Mammy had me well warned not to be running off with 'one of them men in skirts' as she referred to them. Fat chance, I couldn't be bothered with the effort, long busy shifts provided me with enough work, the last thing I wanted to be doing was chasing after a man as well.

My best friend Samantha couldn't understand it. From the second we met on our very first day at Queen Margaret University she had assured me she was going to marry a doctor. Nobody else would do, she was unnervingly certain of what she wanted out of this life. She was born to be a midwife, blessed with a sensitive soul and a determination to help any kind of wounded or wronged living being, be it a tiny bird or a fourteen stone woman in labour. Her compassion was enviable, her patience was endless. She even looked like a doctor's wife, with dark shoulder length bobbed hair and cat-like emerald eyes, the stereotypical girl next door, complete with a sparkling personality and the dirtiest of laughs.

Over the years we had shared the trials and tribulations that student midwifery had thrown at us, the initial shock of working the graveyard shifts, the first delivery, the worst deliveries, the exams, dissertations and everything in between. She had indeed found her doctor, Simon Sanderson, Consultant Obstetrician in the very hospital we worked in. His card was marked the first time she laid eyes on him, everything she had dreamed of in a man; intelligent, kind, compassionate and funny. It was as though she had written a letter describing what she wanted to The Universe and it had been delivered exactly to her specification. Thankfully the feeling was mutual and two years later she had an enormous Tiffany rock securely positioned on the third finger of her left hand and although they were yet to set a date, it wouldn't be long.

She wanted the whole hog, a ridiculously over the top wedding, the enormous tier upon tier of iced wedding cake, the big house and the little babies. Luckily for her it appeared she was on track for it. Samantha was the complete opposite to me in that respect, she couldn't wait to settle down with the right man and have a family of her own.

The thought of settling down terrified me if I was honest. I imagined myself stuck in my hometown of Kinvarra, a gold band on my finger and an enormous bump weighing me down, literally and figuratively. Being surrounded by the same faces I'd known my entire life, the same people doing the same things. I shivered involuntarily thinking about it. The anonymity of the city appealed to me, as did the endless choice of amenities.

Daragh Dunleavey had been my first boyfriend and I had absolutely loved the bones of that boy. I blushed remembering our first summer together; the very same summer that Mary Murphy showed me the direction my life would take. I was torn implacably between staying at home with my first love and moving forward with my ambition to experience city life, to pursue a career in midwifery now that my eyes had been opened.

Daragh was a home bird and as much as I loved him at the time, the reality was that my wandering feet had become more of a priority than my heart. We were so young, too young, it would never have lasted. In the beginning we'd tried to maintain a long distance relationship, he came to Edinburgh every third or fourth weekend when I was a new student midwife. Slowly but painfully we had grown worlds apart. It had been absolutely heart breaking calling it a day, but there hadn't really been any other option.

Over the last ten years I'd bumped into him a few times on one of my infrequent trips home and it tugged viciously at my heart strings, not that I'd admit that to anyone other than Samantha. I couldn't help but feel a slight stirring of envy when I think about him fathering children to another woman as he had since done. Whatever it is about 'the first love', it seemed to leave a permanent mark, branded like a soldered wound on to the heart.

On this particular Friday night, I was out with my colleagues in the City that I had grown to love. I glanced around the busy bar, jostling through the throng of sweaty bodies in an attempt to get the attention of one of the four bartenders on duty. There were many familiar faces, some that I knew exceptionally well, others who I'd met in the hospital corridors in passing. A ridiculous number of us had gathered in one of our favourite drinking haunts, Tonic, a cocktail bar on George Street, for one of the Obstetricians leaving night.

Charlie was one of the Consultants we had come to know well

throughout our training and he was one of the best in the country, hence his services had been sought elsewhere. Through our years of training and for a long time after, he mentored us, listened to countless troubles and tears, offered endless support and guided us solidly through some of our more challenging deliveries. Nothing ever fazed him, the situation could be life or death as it so frequently was on Labour Ward, never once had I witnessed him break a sweat or ruffle a feather. Not even when terrifyingly, we had delivered a baby with the umbilical cord wrapped around his neck, almost suffocating before being whisked off, his tiny face purple, to the Neonatal Ward by two Paediatrician's and three nurses. Nor when a woman delivered her baby in the hospital lift, unable to make it the final few steps to the ward, her waters had spontaneously ruptured on the floor of the hospital entrance below.

Charlie Chadwick was one of those rare men whose intelligence was almost intimidating, his natural IQ out of this world, his experience vast. But the fact that he liked to wear my Clinique Camisole Plump & Shine lip gloss on weekends brought the reality home, he was in fact only human like the rest of us. I caught his eye across the room as one of the particularly handsome SHO's approached him with a rum and coke and I wiggled my eyebrows suggestively at him. He would be greatly missed not only as a mentor but also as a friend.

Despite the cold starry night outside, the room was stifling, my long auburn hair clung to the back of my neck above my fitted black dress. Five inch heels gave me a lift that I didn't necessarily need but after wearing a uniform all week it felt great to make an effort. I wiped a stray bead of perspiration from my porcelain skin and prayed I passed for 'dewy' as opposed to sweaty.

There were three people in front of me, queuing for a drink and I resigned myself to the fact that I could be waiting a while. Bob Sinclair's 'Love Generation' blasted over the carefully positioned speakers and a steady hum of conversation filled the air. A distinctly optimistic Friday feeling radiated promisingly from almost every person in the room, something I was delighted to be a part of for once. When you were a slave to shift work, a weekend off was akin to a week's holiday.

Now next in line, I pointedly looked at my silver watch, the barman nodded at me and lifted his index finger to acknowledge he was coming to me momentarily.Glasses of extravagant cocktails seemed to delay the process and I thought to myself that people should order them by the jug and get on with it. I sighed deeply and battled not to stare at the guy next to me, who's every inch I was fully aware of, despite my best efforts not to be.

'A bottle of Moet please.' I asked and he looked relieved at my simple request.

I'd learnt to appreciate the finer things in life, with the help of my more cultured friends who were waiting patiently at a table in the window for me to return with the next round.

'Hey.' The guy slid into the bar area next to me, his hip pressed lightly against mine as he fought to position his arm territorially onto the bar. I glanced in mild irritation at the nuisance infiltrating my personal space whilst I poorly attempted to negotiate the bottle, glasses and my handbag in one trip. He was good looking at least, I had to give him that. At six foot two he comfortably stood several inches taller than me, with broad shoulders and an athletic physique, he wouldn't have looked out of place in Murrayfield Stadium. His slim fitting suit displayed the strong contours of his body, I willed myself not to stare unsuccessfully. A man that good looking could not be good news.

His full lips parted into a small smile displaying perfectly straight, white teeth as though he were a mind reader and he appeared to mock me. A turquoise tie around his neck emphasised the colour in his enormous ultramarine eyes that crinkled as he broke out into a full grin, hinting he was possibly a few years older than me.

'Hey.' I said, smiling back politely but with professed disinterest. The Streets song 'Fit But You Know It' flicked to the forefront of my mind and I stifled my own giggle. Still, there was no denying he was gorgeous. The subtle scent of his citrus cologne taunted my nostrils as he leaned in to speak again.

I'd passed him in the hospital a few times in the previous couple of weeks but without any real knowledge of who he was or what he was doing there. Someone so attractive couldn't go unnoticed, especially in such a particularly well fitting suit. I might not be looking for marriage, but I was only human.

'You're looking well.' He said confidently into my ear, his breath tickling the sensitive skin of my exposed neckline. I met his eyes evenly, feeling a burning intensity exuding from his stare. I was left in absolutely no doubt that he was flirting with me. Most men didn't bother, apparently I tend to radiate the impression that I'm unavailable, so Samantha frequently informed me.His eyes took in the length of me.

'I suppose you don't look too bad yourself.' I replied evenly, allowing my eyes to deliberately descend lightly over his body, before returning to meet his eye defiantly.

He laughed, a good hearty belly laugh.

'Galway girl?' He said, delighted to be able to pin point my accent.

'Dublin?' I challenged him back, he wasn't the only one who could pin point an accent.

'Touché, well observed.' He laughed again and I couldn't help but join in. We Irish infiltrated every nook and cranny so I wasn't surprised to discover he was a fellow Paddy.

'You're one of the midwives right?' He asked, his initial arrogance replaced with a more appealing natural curiosity upon discovering our mutual heritage.

'You have it in one.' I reply collectedly. As gorgeous as he was, I wasn't one of those women that would simply fall at his feet, as

I'm sure a man with his presence must be well accustomed to.

'What's your story? I've seen you lurking around the hospital.'

'Ah so you've noticed me?' He teased, with borderline arrogance again.

'I hate to have to be the one to tell you this but in a hospital predominantly filled with women either in scrubs, or with a gigantic bump, you stand out like an undertaker in that suit.' It was too tempting not to burst his bubble, he was so confident, seemingly so self-assured.

'Ouch. You've got quite the sharp tongue lady! Be careful you don't cut yourself!' He laughed at my blatant diss. I stuck my tongue out playfully at him.

'I work for a fund management company, I'm a Financial Advisor. We're currently conducting an audit of the financial status of twenty two selected hospitals throughout the UK and Ireland. Someone way up in the food chain is trying to cut costs again somewhere along the line.' He informed me.

'Great, something to look forward to, more staff shortages on the cards. It's getting beyond a joke.' But still, I didn't come out tonight to talk about the current situation within the NHS.

'Not necessarily, but something's going to have to give.' He said seriously.

'On that note…' I gestured to the bottle of champagne I had promised the girls I would return shortly with.

'I'll be around for another few weeks.' He informed me cheekily as I turned away.

'Enjoy yourself.' I replied, refusing to take the bait he was so obviously dangling in front of me. A man of his composure couldn't be good news and I wasn't prepared to find out.

'Great to meet you, Galway.' He nicknamed me casually after

my home town, resigned to the fact he was getting nowhere fast. There were plenty of nurses here who would love to give him a tour of the city and probably anything else he might like to experience. It wouldn't be me.

'Have a good night.' I said, returning to the girls. He flashed me that killer smile, dangerously attractive and sharp too. He looked like the type of guy I usually avoided like the plague, but underneath all the bullshit bravado, there was something intriguing about him. I hated to admit the fact that I'd actually liked him.

CHAPTER TWO

—

Saturday 7th November 2015

Weak rays of autumn sunlight flooded through the partially closed, thick grey curtains. I dragged myself out of bed and made my way to the kitchen desperate to quench my thirst, downing a full pint of water barely pausing for breath. The rain bounced thunderously onto the glass of my double glazed sash windows. From the height of the third floor apartment I had a cracking view of the West End of Princes Street, when it wasn't pouring from the heavens at least. Early morning shoppers roamed the streets below, commuters commenced their mundane journeys to work. A few stragglers from last night appeared to be doing the walk of shame in clothes more appropriate for a night club than a morning walk. The department stores already displayed extravagant crimson Christmas themes, in a few short weeks the big wheel would arrive along with the ice rink, wooden huts and make shift stalls offering immeasurably mouth-watering delicacies and traditional mulled wine.

I couldn't wait. I loved Christmas. Last year I'd spent most of the holiday season on the Labour Ward, escaping back to Ireland to bring in the New Year with my crazy extended relations. This year I was off for two whole weeks, having requested leave nine months in advance.

The shrilling ring of my mobile pierced the quiet of my apartment and I sprinted to the bedroom to reach it before it cut off.

'How's the head? I asked Samantha as a greeting.

'Not too bad considering what I put my body through.' She sounded tired, it had been a late night.

'My head is splitting.' I inform her as I scraped around the drawers for a couple of Paracetamol.

'Who was that guy I saw you talking to at the bar? Don't think I didn't notice!' She asked me unashamedly; desperate to see me paired off with somebody, anybody at this stage.

I sighed at the relentless efforts of my best friend who was longing for us to be at the same stage in life, to get married together, to have families together, despite my regular protests of it not really being on my agenda right now.

He was handsome though, she was right about that. And just because I wasn't looking for a husband it didn't mean I couldn't appreciate a good looking man, on the contrary in fact. I could appreciate them more, then not think about them again. Apart from the fact that this time I had thought about him again, almost as soon as I woke up, regrettably.

I tried to answer her question carelessly, the last thing she needed was any encouragement.

'He's some sort of Financial Advisor for the hospital. He managed to wangle along to Charlie's leaving drinks.' I replied casually, poorly disguising my unlikely interest, even from my best friend.

'So, what did he say?' She probed further, hoping for any snippet of information that she could label as promising, although I could have saved her the trouble and told her she was wasting her time.

'He was Irish, he commented on my Galway accent.'

'He did well, you all just sound Irish to me!' Samantha was from London.

'It was a bit of craic.' It was always nice to meet another Paddy, although it helped that he was exceptionally attractive. His demeanour was what really struck a chord with me. There was something interesting about him, beneath his cocky exterior I was almost certain I glimpsed a flicker of something deeper in his indecently captivating eyes. But that didn't mean I wanted to line him up for marriage.

'What's the plan for today?' Samantha asked yawning lazily down the line, satisfied now that she had settled her curiosity.

'Want to get some lunch? We could meet on Princes Street, do a bit of shopping?' I suggested.

It was one of our favourite ways to spend our free time, wandering aimlessly around the city, shopping leisurely, stopping for a glass of wine in a glass fronted bar where we could admire the view of the majestic castle towering on the hill above us. Its grand demeanour was enchanting, impossible not to appreciate its beauty, the history it boasted. It had stood proudly there for so many years and will do long after we're gone. In winter the dark set in about four o'clock, a lilac glow surrounded the castle, its walls magical in their appearance, a perfect setting for a fairy tale if you believed in them.

'Perfect.' She agreed. Simon was working so I had her to myself for the day.

'I'll grab a shower and meet you at twelve. Text Rebecca and check if she's still alive, she was necking shots like there was no tomorrow.' I said as I poured myself another glass of water, leaning against the sink for support.

Rebecca had been pelvic thrusting around the bar, she had everyone around her in stitches, a natural born entertainer. She was probably in the absolute horrors today, riddled with the drink related anxiety that she suffered so chronically with.

She was our other best friend, the third musketeer, the Scottish one. We were like those jokes that began, 'There was an Englishman, an Irishman and a Scots Man,' apart from the fact that we were women, each representing a different country. Occasionally we encountered cultural differences which made us laugh and simultaneously enlightened each of us in different ways. We were three peas in a pod, complimenting one another's affable personality traits, bound unbreakably by the highs and lows of a career that we had embarked on together.

I stood up from the cream leather sofa I'd slumped on to prepare for the day ahead. Yawning, I stretched my arms out above my head, my back clicking. Padding down the corridor to the main bathroom, past the second bedroom I heard the gentle thud of the post dropping onto the tiles behind me.Swivelling round on my heels, I bent over to pick up three envelopes. Taking them into bathroom, I switched the power shower on, turning my attention to the first envelope while I waited for the water to run hot.It contained a flyer for the Annual Midwifery Conference which was to be held in London next month. I fully intended to go, they were normally great fun and it was an overdue excuse to catch up with some of the girls that had moved away after graduation.

The second letter was a bank statement revealing that I actually had money left over at the end of last month which was a first. A smile played on my lips. Harvey Nicks here we come! Since I'd arrived in the city, I'd developed a penchant for 'fancy make up' as Mammy called it. She loved to inspect the contents of my cosmetics case on my infrequent trips home, smothering herself in my perfume and blusher.

The third envelope was hand written. I recognised the writing but couldn't place it, it was vaguely familiar. A powerful negative instinct rippled through the pit of my stomach as I fingered the envelope, examining it for any clue as to who the sender could be. After turning it over in my hands a couple of times I ripped it open to scan the contents.

Nausea overwhelmed me as I struggled to process the words written on the A4 lined paper, legs buckling beneath me. I collapsed onto the toilet seat, hands trembling, my eyes filled with tears of utter disbelief, I don't shock easily. My upbringing was eventful, my teenage years colourful and between those experiences and my time served on the Labour Ward, and I like to think of myself as fairly steady. The realisation of the identity of the writer winded me.

'Holy Mother of God.' The Catholic curses which usually have the girls in stitches, flew off my lips as I reread the note. Unfortunately it appeared it was time to address issues that we had all been avoiding for years, elements of the past that had been buried for many years. A lot of the time I succeeded in forgetting them, locking them in a chest in the attic space of my subconscious. It was inevitable that it would catch up with me at some point. These things had an ugly habit of rearing their heads when things were just beginning to go smoothly.

The letter fell out of my shaking hands onto the floor, the shower still running next to me. The tears flowed freely, rolling down my face one after another, tears of pent up rage and sorrow, tears that I had forgotten I had.

Oncology
Galway City Hospital
Galway
Wednesday 4ᵗʰ November

Orla,

Don't throw this letter away. I know you probably hate me. I can't say I blame you. I have been selfish in my life and for that girl, I'm sorry.

It's not enough. Nor ever will be, I know.

Is it too much to ask you to give me one more chance?

It's the very last chance for both of us Pet. The years have eventually caught up with me.

I don't want your sympathy, I'm not asking you to care for me while I'm sick. I'd want to see you one more time. To apologise. To see the woman my little girl grew into.

I'd like to see you. But I will never hold it against you if you can't.

You're always in my thoughts Orla.

Dad

CHAPTER THREE

—

Sunday 8th November 2015

He was here, towering in over me, most of his hair had fallen out and the few strands remaining were lank and greasy on his head. His body was weak, black rings circled his eyes, his complexion ashen grey. His voice was rasping, his mouth dry, a result of the chemo. 'Orla' he croaked.

His breath reeked of whiskey despite the health problems he was so obviously encountering. Walking through the front door of my apartment he attempted to embrace me, his touch was weak, a shadow of his former self. My heart hammered in my chest, sweat ensured my clothes were stuck tightly to me. I wasn't sure I was ready for this but I didn't have much choice, he had come for me as I always knew he would one day.

'Daddy.' I eventually uttered. The word that had meant so much to me, but had in reality amounted to very little.I sobbed, huge rolling tears of sorrow and regret, crying for the good times, for the bad. So much time wasted, for what? My body wracked with the overwhelming pain of my emotions and that was what eventually woke me, panting in a cold sweat, in the darkness of my own bedroom.

I flew out of bed, straight to the front door. It was locked, there was nobody here, nobody but me. The city was eerily silent outside the windows, inside my heart hammered in my chest alarmed by the vivid reality of the dream.

Pulling my dressing gown around me protectively, I crept back into the warmth of my bed in an attempt to gather my thoughts. The weekend was like The Never Ending Story, every hour seemed to pass so slowly, I could literally feel the slow, regular ticking of an old Grandfather clock, not yet ready to confront what I knew I needed to do. But it was Sunday night already, time refused to halt for the living.

After my initial shock I'd managed to pull myself together enough to meet up with Samantha as arranged. Her advice was always the first I sought in any situation, the good, the bad or the ugly. Her upbringing wasn't exactly straight forward either, having found out at sixteen upon the untimely death of her mother, that her parents had actually adopted her when she was only a year old. Samantha's biggest issue with the whole thing was that they hadn't told her. And now she could never discuss it with her mother as she had sadly passed away. So many questions that would remain unanswered, yet she managed to deal with it.

On Saturday we strolled around the City for hours, walking companionably, exchanging a few words on occasion and both drowning in the depths of our own thoughts. Samantha's silence was comfortable, it was the noise in my head that wasn't. The questions whirred continuously in my brain as I toyed with the unappealing prospect of returning to Galway to face feelings I had avoided for years. Life had been going so smoothly and for the first time in years I felt settled; I had the security of a permanent job and my very own home. This latest crisis was going to cause turmoil in Kinvarra, I could feel it. It would drag up the past just when Mammy was settled and actually daring to enjoy her happiness.

On Saturday evening as we had watched the embarrassing X Factor hopefuls blaring loudly from the television, I couldn't distract myself even momentarily from that niggling anxiety burning the lining of my stomach. What concerned me most was that this would inevitably bring up everything that Mammy had worked so hard to put behind her. We'd all worked so hard to move on.

I couldn't help but wonder, what kind of cancer? Was it terminal? What if it was already too late? What if I'd already missed him? In a way, a sick part of me for a split second half hoped it were true, purely for the fact that the decision would have been taken out of my hands.I silently chide the cowardly part of myself. The letter was dated only last week, it wouldn't be that quick.

Lying awake staring at the ceiling into the early hours of the morning, I dreaded the thought of breaking it to Mammy and Jack. Although I had to wonder if my brother probably already knew. He always tried to keep an eye on our father from a distance, occasionally making the effort to go for a pint with him, even if it meant at times not being entirely truthful to the rest of us. As I tossed and turned under the warmth of the bed covers I worried about how Mammy would react, I've thrown some gems at her in the past, but this topped them all. The optimistic part of me wondered if maybe she'd encourage me to see my father and make amends before it's too late. Yet on the other hand I wouldn't blame her if she tried to ban me from going near him completely. She is a proud woman, it took her a lot to rebuild her life, to get past what he did to us.

He left her stranded with two young children, a ridiculous amount of debt and more than just bruises on her heart to explain. Rarely had he been seen or heard from since, unless it was to ask for a loan for the horses or to berate her for marrying another man. It had taken years to get her life back. Divorce hadn't even been made legal in Ireland, it was a taboo subject, dividing our own tiny Catholic community, despite the fact the neighbours had often witnessed the horrific scenes around our house. People chose to turn a blind eye. It was a man's world. Thankfully things had moved on in twenty five years, although Breda carried the weight of all that she'd been through in her heart. The last thing she said to him was that she never, ever wanted to see him again, every time he showed up it took her months to get over it again. Because despite everything, she had still loved him, that much was obvious, even to a blind man.

18

CHAPTER FOUR

Monday 9th November 2015

Eventually I must have fallen back into a dreamless sleep, when I looked at the clock it was six am on Monday morning. I switched the alarm on my phone off as it charged on the bedside table next to me, resisting the immediate temptation to hit snooze. Starting four twelve hour shifts on the trot is no joke.

I woke up ignorantly blissful, ready for the day, my only concern that I was feeling kind of sleepy, until the memory of the situation hit me like an oncoming train. Anxiety coursed throughout my veins as I struggled with what exactly I was supposed to do in this scenario.

Showering on autopilot, I dried myself, got dressed, made the bed and toasted a bagel. Twisting my long unruly auburn hair into a clip securely on the back on my head, I slid a few Kirby grips in to tame the stray curls. The routine is so familiar to me I got lost in it for a while, absorbed with the time constraints that I set myself. Routine was important to me on my best days, let alone the harder ones. It supplied me with a feeling of structure and control. Pushing all thoughts of anything else out of my mind I tried to focus solely on the task at hand, but my current crisis continued to niggle at me.

I attempted to concoct an image of him in my mind, what he might look like now, I wondered if I would I even recognize him. Maybe he'd look the same except older, greyer, or heavier with age. It was going to be a long day. I had an awful habit of burying my head in the sand, but I promised myself tonight I would phone Mammy and just tell her. It came as a surprise to me that the whole of Kinvarra didn't already know.

Heading out the door I made my way to the hospital to start my first shift of the week. Arriving on the Labour Ward, the night staff going over the handover in one of the unoccupied Labour Suites, I strain hard to listen to the Consultant speaking about each of the Mum's in our care. There are currently four women on the ward, one of whom is waiting for the Anaesthetist, another who just received a shot of Pethidine, one who is almost nine centimetres dilated and almost ready to go. The last woman was currently sitting in one of our NHS bog standard baths trying to ease her contractions naturally. He dismissed us and allocated us a patient each.

After all that I had seen in my experience on Labour Ward, if I ever did decide to have children, (and that is an enormous IF), one thing was certain, I'd be taking all the drugs available. What women went through was something else. The more I think of Mary Murphy that momentous day, the more respect I have for her. They certainly didn't call it labour for nothing.

Taking the clinical notes with me for the Mum in four, I pinned on my name tag and knocked on the door before entering. Inside was a big boned, strong woman wearing an oversized man's checked shirt and nothing else. She crouched on the bed on all fours rocking back and forth through the contractions, she was what we called a Multip, meaning it wasn't her first baby. She was experienced at this stage and it showed. Her husband sat next to her on the standard battered hospital arm chair. He too was a big man, burly broad shoulders with a broad Edinburgh accent to go with it.

'You're doing great lass.' He assured her, nodding proudly at his wife.

I washed my hands thoroughly in the sink before the girl I was taking over from, Liz, introduced me.

'This is Orla. She is going to be taking over from me now.'

They barely looked up, so engrossed in the situation they were in. I snapped on a pair of gloves to examine Mum as Liz wished them well and said goodbye. These days I thought absolutely nothing of where I had to push my fingers, it was second nature, came with the job description. It wasn't for the squeamish or the faint hearted. We have seen many Dads hit the deck when the shit hit the fan, many of them just not cut out for watching labour.

Sometimes at the end of a long shift, the Mum begged you not to leave, they'd spent twelve of the hardest hours of their life with you by their side as a safety blanket. We weren't technically supposed to stay. Occasionally I couldn't help it, drawn in, compelled to finish what I'd started. It was difficult to leave when you had invested so much. Especially with what we call the Prims, the first time Mum's, or following the instance of a Rainbow Baby, as they were now referred to. In these circumstances, there was something that compelled me to ensure these couples got their happy ending following a tragedy. I needed to witness it for myself as much as for them.

'Okay Mum, you are so close, but you know that yourself. You're doing absolutely brilliantly. A natural.' We called all the women 'Mum.' It was easier and if they weren't already used to it by now, they were about to get used to it pretty quickly.

I check the monitor displayed next to the bed thoroughly, all looked well. The lady wore a CTG belt to trace the baby's heart rate. Sometimes towards the end of the labour the baby's heart rate can drop as they tire or increase rapidly as they become distressed. This particular baby was cool as a cucumber, no panic here thank God.

'What do you have at home?' I asked Dad.

'Two boys, aged four and two.' He replied barely taking his eyes from his wife.

'Busy house.' I acknowledged, remembering the days I used to babysit Mary Murphy's brood of boys.

A short while later, with minimal fuss, Mum delivered a nine pound, eight ounce baby boy, naturally I might add, aided only by gas and air. She didn't tear, not even a millimetre. Some women were born to bear children and this lady was one of them. It was one of the simplest deliveries I'd had the pleasure of attending to in my ten years, probably a saving grace because try as I might, I was a little distracted. A hospital was definitely not a place to be distracted.

I found myself looking at these two parents, gazing at their gorgeous new son adoringly, as if he were the only thing in the world right now, trying to imagine if Mammy and Daddy had looked at us like that when we were born. Was Daddy even there? I'd never thought to wonder before, although I doubted it. Twenty eight years ago the Labour Ward was no place for any man, it would have be unheard of. In fact knowing how backwards things are in rural Ireland I'd be surprised if many men accompanied their wives as they delivered their children even now.

Daddy was probably wetting his child's head with a few jars from the barrel in the local. It was a man's world. How Mammy ever ended up married to my father is beyond me. She was strong, sensible, firm but fair. One thing I do know is that she loved him, oh how she had loved him.

Around midday I made my way to the canteen for a quick cup of tea, I had zero appetite but I'd have to try. It could be a long day on the feet in St. Margaret's. Rebecca sat at a table with her sandwich in front of her a bottle of water. It was rare we actually got a lunch, let alone together.

'How are you Orla?' She asked gently, motioning towards the seat next to her.

'Okay I guess.' I shrugged and she gave my arm a supportive squeeze.

I helped myself to a tea bag, placed the white cup under the machine and pressed the button for hot water. I deliberately changed the subject, glancing around the room at our colleagues and friends.

'This place seems quiet without Charlie already.' I said.

'He'll be back. Mark my words, Glasgow Maternity Hospital doesn't have the same charm as this place.' Rebecca replied with a mouthful of chicken mayo.

Our table was the same one we always tried to get, next to the door so we could observe the comings and goings of our peers. Maybe I had brought more of Kinvarra over with me than I had initially thought!

Rebecca chatted with two theatre nurses at the table next to us about Charlie's leaving night and Samantha joined us briefly just as we were finishing up. The lady she had been assigned to, a Prima, had had a particularly hard time of it by all accounts. Samantha only had five minutes and she had to go straight back up to complete the pile of paperwork involved and check how the feeding was going. We had an on-site Lactation Consultant if needed and we always tried to encourage the Mum's to at least try breast feeding even if they weren't initially keen.

Sam squeezed into the tight space next to the wall sitting practically on top of me, if it were anyone else it would be an invasion of privacy, but from my best friend it was comfort at its best.

'You alright chick?' She asked sympathetically.

'I'm okay. Any craic?'

'Not yet but the day is young.' Samantha's eyes twinkled with mischief as she stared blatantly over my shoulder. I felt a swift hard kick to my ankle underneath the dinner table.

'Ouch!' I exclaimed. 'What was that for?' If it was supposed to take my mind off things, it had worked, temporarily.

She nodded in the direction behind me and raised her eyebrows suggestively.

The Dub, as I had named him, from Friday night strode confidently into the canteen, whistling to himself under his breath. I couldn't decide if he was arrogant, confident or merely oblivious to his own outrageous appeal. As he helped himself to a coffee from the recently fitted state of the art machine, my eyes ran up and down the length of him. In the light of day, he was equally as attractive, traffic stopping, even jaw dropping. Once again, I tried not to stare but it was almost impossible. I was loathsome to admit that in the last ten years there hadn't been a man that stirred this type of ridiculous lust in me.

His broad shoulders, a complete contrast to his narrow waist, were displayed beautifully in a slim fitting navy suit and white shirt. Indecently chiselled features sat perfectly in proportion on his tanned face, his piercing eyes were startling against his dark complexion. He didn't get that tanned in this country that was for sure. My insides somersaulted at the sight of him, recalling that not only was he attractive, but funny and charming in addition, possibly too charming. It couldn't be healthy.

'Isn't that the guy you were talking to on Friday night Orla? In Tonic?' Rebecca chipped in, oblivious to the kick I'd already received.

That was him alright. In practically a different life time. Before the letter. My mind wondered back to our conversation at the bar. He hadn't exactly asked me out, but he had definitely suggested something to that effect. It was a tempting thought, even more so because his position in Edinburgh was only temporary, which suited my inability to maintain an actual relationship. Although it was hard to imagine he was a man looking for a serious relationship, from the ease in which his suggestive remarks left his lips, he most certainly had experience in approaching women. The least sensible part of me gazed dreamily at his backside for a few brief seconds, a harmless distraction, my eyes lingered over his powerful shoulders and perfectly formed butt.

Crashing back to reality with a startling racket, I managed

to knock over my cup of tea, the remaining mucky brown liquid splashing all over the table, unfortunately attracting the attention of The Dub, for all the wrong reasons. He winced at the clattering crockery before breaking into a devilish grin as he realised the source of it. He winked cheekily and the blush crept into my porcelain cheeks, giving me away, if my megawatt beam hadn't already. It was the first real smile I'd managed all weekend.

'It was him you were talking to wasn't it Orla?' Rebecca asked again, mopping up the spillage with a napkin, oblivious to the increasing shade of crimson I was turning.

'Yes, it was him.' He really was striking, he had to know it. Totally not my type, I reminded myself. Reluctantly I had to admit in the light of day, without the armour of my make up, he had me flustered.

Then I remembered the new found family crisis that had since emerged to bite me in the ass. I was in absolutely no position to be eyeing up some random, albeit indecently attractive stranger when I have enough of my own shit to deal with. It was inappropriate.

Samantha must have read my mind. 'Let's get back up to the Ward. Some poor women probably need all the help they can get right now! And I'm talking about the other Midwives!' She said in jest, but we knew all too well the truth of the situation, short staffed wasn't the word for it.

'Don't think I missed that less than private exchange.' Samantha whispered as we headed back up to the Labour Ward, linking arms conspiratorially. She clearly hadn't abandoned her hopes of pairing me off with the first unsuspecting man who took a serious interest. I couldn't imagine it would be him, even if I wanted it to be, which I didn't, I reminded myself.

The day passed with one more delivery and one false alarm, Braxton Hicks – practice contractions often mistaken for the beginnings of labour. It was hard to concentrate fully, something I couldn't afford in here. Ridiculously perhaps, I'd never dreamed that I'd come up against the situation at home. A part of me always thought Daddy would drink himself to death alone somewhere; that we'd get a phone call one day to say he had passed.

Could he really have stopped drinking after all these years? The letter was coherent, well thought out. Although Alcoholics are often some of the best actors in the world, primarily because they had to be. It was hard to see the light through my complicated emotional state. It felt a bit like ripping the plaster off a wound that had almost healed. It was all coming back to me in fragmented pieces, the endless times he promised to come to my birthday parties, to take me to get my new school uniform, to make the Christmas play.

Each and every time he assured me, this time would be different. I'd believed him so desperately because I wanted to, only to be let down each time. The late nights he hammered on the door stinking of alcohol, demanding to know if Mammy had a man in the house. She soon got smart and phoned The Guards from then on, desperately trying to ignore the fists pounding on the solid wood, turning the television on in a poor attempt to disguise the noise from her children. I'll never forget how tried to shelter us from it.

One time he threw a brick through the window which hurtled into the back of my Mams head, resulting in a trip to the surgery. My brother and I sat on the carpet in the lounge, the shattered glass from the window in our hair and under our feet, fragments of tiny shards scattered amongst our toys. Mammy did her best to protect us from it, and herself.

Then years later she met Patrick. Patrick was seven years older than Mam, a carpenter, originally from Cork. Patrick is a kind man, they have been married for six years now and couldn't be happier. It was a relief to know she was settled, Patrick took care of her. Selfishly, it eased my own guilt of being away from home.

Of course, it wasn't always that way, I had fond memories of Daddy too. Once he brought my brother and I a book home each following a week of absence (no doubt on a bender). He sat us on each of his knees and read to us patiently on the occasions that he actually arrived home, the smell of whiskey and tobacco fresh on his breath. As toddlers he brought us to the pier in Kinvarra to teach us how to swim, despite the freezing cold temperatures, he insisted it would toughen us up for later on in life. We used to go every week for a while, when he wasn't drinking. Once he'd taken his eye off the ball for few seconds. I asked Jack what he thought would happen if I put my armbands on my ankles, I was a curious child. Jack shrugged his shoulders not all that interested in his baby sister's ramblings. I decided to find out for myself first hand; I swallowed a lot of water that day. Daddy rescued me from drowning, dragging me to the safety of the shore coughing and spluttering. It had been years since I'd thought of that particular day.

With memories such this one influencing my heart of hearts, I'd never be able reach any other conclusion. I had to see my father before it's too late.

CHAPTER FIVE

—

Tuesday 10th November 2015

I dialled the number automatically, not even thinking about it. Most days I phone home as soon as I get in from work for a quick chat with Mammy. She's a worrier, she liked to know I was still alive. Over the last ten years she's visited Edinburgh countless times yet still manages to get lost on the three main streets, complaining at every opportunity that the traffic and the noise is unbearable. I'm sure she thinks if she says it enough, eventually I'll realise it too and come home.

The bleeping tone alerts me to the fact the call is being connected. Mammy talks. A lot. It seems very Irish to me now, living in Scotland I can't help but notice what Samantha calls my 'Irish-isms'. Quite often I don't get a word in edgeways as she repeats the comings and goings of each and every single one of the neighbours before she rushes off, with the mandatory five thousand 'Bye, bye, bye, bye, bye, Good Luck! Bye!'

Today is no different, except that it is.

Patrick answers. '867922'

Why do people do that? Anyone phoning you would clearly be aware of the number they have dialled! They both do it now, Mam and Patrick, it's hilarious. It's like something out of the nineteen twenties when phone lines had only just been introduced. I mean can you imagine if everyone answered their mobiles '07738789440.' It would be bizarre.

'Patrick, how are you?' Even though Patrick is the closest thing I have really had to a Dad I'd never have dreamed of calling him Daddy, because he's not, nor ever will be, despite the fact he is married to my mother. But I usually call Mam 'Breda' if we are in company. Being called by her Christian name makes her feel young again, one of the girls.

'Orla. I'm grand! Any craic from the big smoke?' The sound of Patrick's familiar Cork accent was therapeutic to my anxious soul. I closed my eyes for a few seconds, pretending I stood next to him, a fraction of the tension in my shoulders eased. I wanted to spill everything out there and then, but it was only fair that I told Mammy first.

'Ah, you know the usual, work night out on Friday and then X-Factor on Saturday Patrick, you know what it's like'. He probably didn't. I skipped over the finer details anyway.

'Sure, I'll put your Mammy on the phone, she'll be dying to talk to you. Take care of yourself Orla, hope to see you soon.' That was a niggling reminder that I hadn't been home since April. Careful what you wish for Patrick, looks I'll be home sooner than you could imagine.

I could hear him hollering up the stairs, 'Pick up the phone in the bedroom, it's Orla for you'.

I hear a click and a familiar voice shouts down the stairs back to him, 'I've got it!' deafening us both in one ear.

'Hi Pet, how are you now?'

I reply with 'Mammy, I'm okay how are you?'

'It's been a busy day down at the surgery, you know what it gets like in there, absolute madness on a Monday always….' Mammy had switched her job as a home help for a receptionist role in our local surgery when she had been diagnosed with epilepsy three years ago and given up her driver's licence.

'You wouldn't believe who came in today!' She continued, the tone of her voice pitching at an excited all-time high. Before I even had a chance to open my mouth to reply she continued without pausing for breath.

'Daragh Dunleavey's girlfriend! And she's pregnant again! Mind you, you've not to repeat that…of course you won't anyway, I didn't even need to say that! Can you believe it though? That'll be the third baby in so many years! You'd think that boy would have married her by now! Sure look, I hope he doesn't think he's hanging on for you!'

Mam could talk the hind leg off a donkey, and its arse and belly too.I tuned back in to hear her saying 'And I can't help but look at those kids and think they could have been yours! I could have been a Grandma!'

That sentence makes me wince, it is a thought I have occasionally stumbled across myself, not that I would admit that to her. So far as anyone else was concerned I didn't want children, not that it was any of their business, but it was easier to just put that out there first before anyone tried to embarrass me with the, 'Are you still single?' question that I loathed every time I returned home.

'Mammy! You know it would never have worked out, I had to leave, I had itchy feet which is something Daragh didn't seem to have a problem with at all!'

I try and round up that line of conversation as quickly as possible in order to address the real issue at hand, but she continues on relentlessly.

'I see his Mammy sometimes, she's not married to his father anymore, oh no, she's got the right idea. She's only gone and got herself a toy boy! You'll never guess who he is!'

She's right about that anyway, I wouldn't guess, because I don't actually care. But I wait patiently until she gets to the end of her story out of respect for the fact that she is Mammy and I am the dutiful daughter that just happens to live in another country.

'It's only Susan McCowan's second cousin! Sue says she's onto a winner with that one, apparently he's got his own property management business or something.'

I grunted in acknowledgement and cleared my throat, in preparation to break the news about Daddy.

'Orla, my dinners going to burn if I don't get it out the oven right now, I'll call you back this evening! After I've watched Corrie, but before EastEnders!'

She always did love her soaps. And just like that she was gone. I stood in the quiet darkness of the lounge still cradling the phone wondering what just happened. Who the hell was Sue anyway?

I'd have to broach the subject later on. I'd reflected enough, I was ready to get it out in the open. What I was really hoping for was to revert back to a childhood state, for someone older, with more experience in these situations to take charge. That way I'd no longer be responsible for any decisions myself. Although I already knew what I was going to do, I briefly acknowledged that it's more likely her approval I seek rather than her advice. Just when life seems to be going swimmingly something like this happens and throws it into turmoil. Talk about a MidWife Crisis!

I realise I'm pacing the lounge and decide to hit the gym to burn off my nervous energy and attempt to clear my mind. Virgin Active is a ten minute walk from my apartment, eight if I'm quick. I should make more of an effort to go, having joined shortly after Hogmanay, resolving to get back to a size ten after a week at home eating everything and anything Breda put in front of me. There was a lot to be said for Mammy's cooking.

As I entered the gym complex the smell of chlorine from the pool hit me, cleansing and welcoming. It was well kitted out with an abundance of modern equipment and the staff were friendly and approachable. It wasn't one of those God awful places that held an inane amount of body building men or skinny selfie taking women. The clientele was vast, from menopausal women to teenagers. I felt oddly comfortable here, like I belonged to something. I admired the shiny doors and the surprising peace and quiet of the corridors and I vowed to come more often. The thought of it was worse than the work out itself. That night I was grateful for the distraction.

Dumping my stuff in the locker I headed to the first treadmill I reached, barely bothering to warm up. I ran, upping the pace forcefully with one finger. After a few minutes my calves burned, my eyes focussed on the plasma on the wall displaying Madonna's video to 'Hung Up on You'.

The devil on my shoulder refused to grant me peace, tormenting me, analysing my feelings and pushing me for answers. What if it's too late already? How ill is he? What does he expect from me after all these years? What would I say to him? Would he even recognise me? I have no idea how to deal with this.

Daddy comes from a big family, like most Irish Catholic households. I hadn't seen his brothers or sister for a long time, several of them still lived in Connemara, where he was originally from, two brothers lived in the City now. By that I mean Galway City. Were they aware? Did they care? He had alienated us all at one point or another.

Five hundred and thirty four calories later I fling a towel round my neck and head to the cross trainer. Still the questions whir, despite the burning of muscles I forgot I had. What will Breda think? Does Jack know? What's the best way to approach this awful situation?

I attempted to fathom every possible scenario but nothing seemed to fit right. The truth of the matter was, I didn't have a clue and the only thing I was certain of is that I needed to tell Mam before somebody else did. I probably should organise some time off work. An hour later I left the gym not bothering to shower, preferring to wash in the comfort of my own home. Out of habit I pulled my iPhone out of my bag, glancing down to see if I had any texts. Five missed calls, three voicemails and two texts. I dialled 901 and the posh English lady introduced my messages.

First Message, message received at seven twenty seven. To return the call press the hash key. Beep 'Orla, its Jack I'm wondering if you could give me a call back as soon as please. It's important.'

Second Message, message received at seven twenty nine. To return the call press the hash key. Beep 'Hi Orla it's only me Mam, where are you? Ring me. It's important.'

Third message, message received at seven forty five. To return the call press the hash key. Beep 'Are you okay? I've tried ringing the flat as well?' Mam again. She's more than a little impatient.

I walk the eight minutes home quickly, it's dark but East Fountainbridge is exceptionally well lit even under a blanket of clouds, the road is always busy with traffic. The landline rings loudly as I turn the key in the front door and step inside out of the cold corridor.

'Hello?' (I do not feel the need to answer the phone with the number the person has just dialled.)

'Orla, its Jack I left you a message I'm not sure if you listened to it yet.'

Jack rarely phones me, preferring the odd text or Facebook meme, tagging me in stupid posts to remind me, 'The oldest sibling is always the best looking' or some other such shite. What I wouldn't do for that easy banter tonight, sadly we had more important things to discuss.

'You got the letter?' He cuts straight to the point, no time to waste.

'I did.' I sigh.

'And, what do you think?' He asks gently.

'I don't know what to think to be honest.' My voice wobbles slightly.

'Orla, the man is dying. I know how you feel, believe me I do,

I was there too. But it's now or never.' He urges me, he always had a soft spot for Daddy. After everything that occurred he continued to chase him for his time and attention.

'As in right now?' I'm shocked at the sudden urgency of the situation.

'He might have weeks if he is lucky. I've been. It doesn't look good.' He says.

'Jack I just…' I don't know what to say.

'Look, you have a few days to think about it. But if you are coming, don't delay. He is desperate to see you.'

'Ok.' I nod, crying silently into the receiver.

'Ok, as in your coming?' He confirms.

'Yes.' I agree before I can change my mind. 'But not until the weekend. I'm working the next three days. I need to get my head straight. See you Saturday.'

'Good girl. I honestly think it's the right thing to do.' Jack is openly relieved. I'm relieved he will be there with me.

'What about Mammy?' I ask him, worried already at what she will say.

'Mammy is fine. She is adamant she's not going. Her exact words were, 'He's a long time dead to me already'. I flinched at the truth of it.

'You'll meet me at the airport?' I plead.

'Of course. It will be okay, I promise. You'll feel better once you've seen him. Closure for everyone.'

I doubted it but I didn't have it in me to argue with him.

'I'll be in touch before the weekend.' He promises.

'Love you.' I say to the empty receiver, he already hung up.

CHAPTER SIX

———

Wednesday 11ᵗʰ November 2015

The next morning I went directly to the Head of my Department and explained the situation. Pauline is an older woman, only three years away from retirement with an abundance of experience under her belt, unsurprising following thirty years on the job.

'Go now Orla. I'll get some of the bank staff to cover your shifts.' She urged me.

'I can't.' I said numbly.

'Why on earth not? Go now while you can. We'll manage here.'

'Just not yet.' I look to the floor eyeing my clinical navy Crocs, concentrating intently on each hole in the rubber, wondering if there was even a remote possibility that I could slither right down through one and disappear until everything blows over.

'Are you okay?' She placed her hand gently on mine in the manner that we usually reserve for nervous patients, leaning in closer to scrutinise my face for a trace of an unspoken answer.

'I'm not ready to go yet. I need a few days to sort my head out. The situation is less than ideal in more than just the obvious sense.' I tried to explain without divulging my entire life story, it would take too long and neither of us wanted to hear it anyway.

'I see.' She nodded curtly, having witnessed enough families passing through these doors over the years, she knew when to leave well alone.

'Well if you're sure? Go any time you need to. Just say the word.' She stood, indicating that our brief meeting was over.

'Thank you. I'll bear it in mind. I might take a few days off down the line.'

'Of course. Do what's right for you Orla.' She tells me kindly as I leave her office.

I would, if only I knew what that was.

There was no time for a lunch break today, one of the other midwives was attending a home birth in Leith and we were operating at maximum capacity. I blamed Samantha, who had committed the all-time midwife feck up, commenting on the fact it was quiet when we arrived to take over from the night shift. Nobody ever mentions the Q word on Labour Ward, ultimately it provokes an overload of admittances, which was exactly what happened shortly before midday. She must have forgotten herself in the excitement of looking at wedding venues last night.

By late afternoon my stomach growled ferociously, Steph covered for me while I snuck out to the vending machine, my lady walking the floors with her husband in an attempt to move things along naturally. I craved sugar and a caffeine rush, it was the only way to get through the day. Slotting loose change into the machine I selected a Twix for myself and a Mars for Steph. As I rushed back up the stairs to the Labour Ward I practically ran into a figure charging down, very nearly emptying my black coffee all over his crisp white shirt.

'Whoa.' He steadied me with a strong hand. The Dub, of course it would have to be wouldn't it?

'Jeez, I'm so sorry.' He'd have me pegged as the clumsiest woman on this earth before the week was out.

'There was me thinking you were the kind of woman that I

36

sent running in the opposite direction, given the way you left me hanging the other night, yet here you are proving me wrong.' He said, his sparkling eyes meeting mine, almost questioningly.

'So sorry. I literally only had two minutes free. Hot coffee is hard to come by up there.' I gestured to the ward above. I was acutely aware that in the madness of this busy hospital, we were alone, temporarily at least. I had his undivided attention, and I liked it.

'Are you ok?' He asked, examining me closer, seeing the tell-tale shadows of the last few sleepless nights. Appearing briefly concerned, his usual borderline arrogance was replaced with a more gentlemanly approach, a manner that was so much more appealing than the earlier bravado.

'Busy.' I said, unable to meet his eye. There was so much more to this week, I hadn't expected him to pick up on it. For a second I opened my mouth to explain, but I caught myself in time. As if he would be interested, I barely knew him. Maybe it was his Irish accent that made me want me to spill all to him, maybe it was the smooth concern of his gentle tone. Either way, it would be dangerous to get too close to a man like him, everything about him screamed heartbreaker. And I wasn't the heart broken type. Mind you, until recently I hadn't been the lusty type either, but this man stirred desires in me that I hadn't realised I'd had locked away inside.

'Well, have a good day.' He said with a resigned look that implied so much more than the simple words he uttered.

I was reluctant to leave him. Unnervingly I was equally as drawn to his self-assured personality as to his obviously masculine physique. Underneath the exterior swagger was a three dimensional puzzle, when he wasn't teasing me, he emitted a genuine warmth that enticed me.I could no longer deny it.

'You too.' I said, as he stepped out of the way allowing me to pass, gently brushing his hand over my arm where my hospital issue navy scrub top stopped above my elbow. Every single hair on my body stood on end in response to his touch. As I reached the top step I turned briefly to take one last mental snapshot of his perfectly formed figure. Apparently he had the same idea. He stood motionlessly at the bottom of the stairs unashamedly admiring the rear view.

The chemistry was painful; it crackled between us, electric in the otherwise still and unusually empty hall. He winked at me appreciatively and a slow smile spread helplessly across my face. He had me and he knew it. But it worked both ways, it would seem we had much more in common than just our heritage; a rising appreciation for each other.

CHAPTER SEVEN

—

Thursday 12ᵗʰ November

Having committed to making the trip that weekend I'd seriously questioned if it was the right thing, if Daddy would be different to the way I remembered him. He couldn't be drunk given the current situation, although not out of choice by all accounts. If the nurses left their alcohol hand rub on the end of his bed he'd probably chance downing that. Anything to escape his awful new reality. Given the latest news, I probably wouldn't blame him.

He was previously a very aggressive, short tempered man, combined with his current illness and the considerable pain he may be in, I wasn't sure if this was a wise idea. Emotionally I was hanging on the edge of a thread waiting to see if I could actually go through with my promise. If the shit hit the fan, I wouldn't hesitate to turn around and walk straight back out the door.

Surely his outlook would have changed following a diagnosis of lung cancer. Jack mentioned he'd had chemotherapy but the Consultant advised it was an attempt to simply prolong his life, it was never offered as a cure. It was far too advanced for that, only in the hands of God now.

I booked an Aer Lingus flight from my mobile phone at lunch time. Jack agreed to pick me up at Knock Airport and take me straight to the Galway Hospital, to face the music before going home to Mammy's house. At least with her I could then hopefully relax a little, with the worst of it over for me. Every cloud has a silver lining, even this dark thunderous one, Breda is over the moon I'm coming home. I really shouldn't have left it so long, it wasn't right.

I'd often found myself in less than ideal situations, left to wonder afterwards how the hell I ended up there in the first place. A prime example is the time that Daragh Dunleavey and I went to the fair when I first arrived back in Kinvarra. I hate roller coasters, detest unpredictable rides, to this day I'm still terrified of heights. If our Lord wanted me to be up high, he would have given me wings. Regardless of this detail, I still found myself sat with my head in the clouds, literally and metaphorically, at the top of a less than secure, travelling tower ride, with only one cheap flimsy bar of metal apparently securing me in position. My legs dangled freely, with nothing but fresh air to support them.

Admittedly the view was fantastic from that great height but the apprehension was too much for me. The icy hands of terror crept around my insides, gripping my palpitating heart tightly, while I waited for the inevitable gut wrenching drop. What goes up must come down. I held my breath for an eternity, eyes shut tightly offering every prayer I could think of to anyone that may potentially hear me. I prayed I wouldn't vomit as we were dropped mercilessly from the sky, at lightning speed to the safety of the damp ground below.

Just when I thought it was all over, daring to briefly open one eye, the blasted thing shot us back into the sky for round two. Once again we plummeted to the ground, butt cheeks clenched, lips pursed, eyes squeezed mercifully shut again to restrain the impending rush of sickness that threatened. In complete contrast to me, Daragh thought it was hilarious. He was easily entertained, fearless, or perhaps without any regard for his life. I vowed never again. I hated rides, hated giddiness, hated heights, why would I put myself in that situation?

I can't help but wonder if I'd just agreed to put myself in one of those dangerously vulnerable situations again, by reuniting with my father. Unfortunately it appeared to be a no win situation, my back pressed to the wall either way.

Mammy was actually fine about everything. Jack had gotten to her first and explained the situation, thankfully saving me that particularly unappealing job. Although she had encouraged me to see Daddy, she made me swear I wouldn't talk about her to him at all, no matter what he asked. She continued to maintain that he was dead to her for a long time already, harsh but true. Whatever he was, we both acknowledged the fact that he would always be my father. When something happened to him, and it was when, not if, she wanted my conscience to be clear and without regret. What she said made sense. For all Mammy's mindless chattering and gossiping, when it came down to it, she was as sharp as a razorblade and as solid as a rock.

I lay in the heat and steam of an Epsom salt bath reflecting on all that had passed and what was yet to come. Fleeting thoughts of The Dub continued to infiltrate my mind despite my best efforts. By all accounts, he wouldn't be around for long, I couldn't establish if that was a good or bad thing, but erred on the side of positivity. After all, even if I was crazy enough to pursue him, it's not like it could develop into anything. I hadn't had a proper relationship since the age of nineteen, nor had I since longed for one. I wasn't the kind of girl that *needed* a man and I'd never met one that I'd actually *wanted* enough to pursue. As my skin shrivelled like a prune under the hot water I concluded it had to be a good thing he wasn't based here permanently, my interest in him unnerved me.

My mobile phone vibrated on the side of the bath and I dried my hand on a nearby towel to pick it up. It was a message from Samantha.

WEDDING BOOKED. S x

My friend, the fast mover. I was desperate to hear the details, delighted Samantha had met someone to settle down with. She's desperately broody despite the fact she's only twenty-seven, adamant she wants four children.

You'd think given the job we do she could have been easily deterred. Women arrived on Labour Ward and left their dignity at the door. It was messy, bloody, raw and agonising. In the end it was usually euphoric but occasionally it could be tragic too. Not all of the cases on the ward ended with a Happily Ever After. Those memories we carried with us in our hearts every single day, soldered onto our souls for the rest of our lives. I can't remember each and every name but I remember their faces, the shattering of their world as the worst possible nightmare became reality.

The majority of cases ended well, thank God. We midwives lived for that perfect moment after the labour, after all the pain, the struggle, the hours of contractions. That moment when the Mum you had been taking care of laid her eyes on her baby, flesh of her flesh, blood of her blood, for the very first time. That was what made it all worthwhile. In that split second, the last few agonizing moments of the delivery, the atmosphere swivels a full one hundred and eighty degrees, from tension, apprehension, agony and anxiety to sheer and utter joyous euphoria for all involved. Us included. That magical moment in which a Mother lays eyes on her precious child for the first time, is comparable to nothing else in the entire Universe.

As a midwife I never ever tire of seeing this absolute wonder of nature, so private, so overwhelming, a privilege to be part of. It truly is magical. An endurance test for all involved, especially the mother. But the raw emotion that followed was indescribable, purer than the strongest of drugs.

Samantha wanted that moment for herself. Sooner rather than later.

Children scare me. Not even the delivery or the labour, but the actual responsibility of having tiny humans to care for forever. People depending on me day and night, I'm not sure I could hack it to be honest. Maybe I'm selfish, or maybe I just haven't got there yet, but I wasn't getting any younger either.

I'd never really thought much about getting married. I was never one of those little girls that walked around with their pillowcase on their head singing 'Here Comes the Bride'. Irish weddings are a big deal, especially where I grew up. When a person got married, the whole town was invited. I've witnessed countless romantic days, yet never once did I long to be the woman in white. It was never on my agenda. I found the thought of tying myself to another person difficult if I was brutally honest, after all the things I witnessed early on with Mammy and Daddy. It's not something I could forget, not that I technically saw much, it was more what I heard, vases being smashed, photo frames being thrown, shouting obscenities and the aching sound of tears of heartfelt sorrow.

Even with my first boyfriend Daragh, I never really imagined marrying him, we were so young, although it wouldn't have been out of the question in Kinvarra. At the time I thought I was in love with him. He was four years older than me, we were together for eight months before I got the opportunity to move to Edinburgh and study Midwifery. I met him a few months before Mrs Murphy burst in on me that day and changed my life forever, providing me with an actual purpose.

We'd been dating, if that's what you could even call it, kissed a few times at the local disco. Then we started hanging out together, he'd pick me up and take me to the cinema in the city once a week, I'd loved the independence of being in the city without Mam watching over me. If the weather was dry, we'd go to the park and talk for hours. Because he was older than me, initially I was in awe of him, he appeared mature and confident. He had a permanent job as a fisherman and his own house. He was already planning for the future. I suppose I was flattered by his attention, feeling barely more than a child myself.

When the letter arrived with the offer of a place to study Midwifery in Edinburgh it was bittersweet for me. I was desperate to get on the course, to chase the waking interest in all things child birth related, but it meant leaving Daragh for the foreseeable future. Leaving a relationship that our tiny town had already proclaimed 'would give them all a day out yet!'

Stupidly, or maybe naively, I thought our relationship was strong enough to go the distance. I was wrong. Daragh's insecurities and probably the difference in our age lead him to develop trust issues, despite the fact I'd never ever given him any reason to doubt me. I'd never been promiscuous; he should have known that better than anybody. He spent months trying to get me to sleep with him, it had taken a lot of persuasion. He was my first. Despite our history he seemed to have forgotten all of this, all rationale escaping him. Our interests changed, mine more so than his, resulting in us drifting apart permanently. It taught me something anyway, long distance relationships don't work.

I stood up and stepped out of the bath, pulling my towel around me, deciding to stop pondering the evening away and actually get organised.It was about time I pulled out my travel case and packed a few things, unsure what would be considered suitable attire for this unusual reunion.Opening my double wardrobe I folded a few smart casual outfits into my tiny hand luggage case; jeans, flat brown leather boots, a couple of shirts and a Ralph Lauren V-neck pullover.

I tried, unsuccessfully, to look on the bright side. It would be nice to see Jack despite the circumstances and Mammy of course. Dread washed over me, vicious cramps attack my stomach. But the decision had been made. I assured myself that I am a grown woman, I know what I'm doing. In reality I hadn't a clue.

CHAPTER EIGHT

—

Friday 13th November 2015

I didn't believe in ridiculous Friday the thirteenth suspicions but I had the distinct feeling it was going to be a tough day on Labour Ward. The morning dawned with the usual shrilling alarm tone rudely awakening me from the deep sleep I had eventually slipped into. We usually do four twelve hour shifts if we are on day shift or three night shifts if we are on graveyard duty, but this was my fifth day in a row. I'd swapped it for a day off the next week, when I more than likely would need it to recover from the trip to Galway.

I imagined I'd hate the graveyard shift as we call it, but the thought of it is worse than when it actually comes around, one week in every month. Most of the time we're too busy to notice what hour of the day it is. Women in labour have no regard for the clock, babies are without the concept of time, arriving when they are ready and not a moment before.

I traipsed into the changing rooms, dumped my bag in my locker, put my lunch into the tiny fridge and changed into the standard 'sexy' navy scrubs, dragging my hair up into a loose pony tail ready for the onslaught of whatever the day may bring. Most of the time it was pure madness.

For some women, there has been so much thought put into this single event in their lives, so much wondering and worrying about what will it be like to actually have a baby, to push a tiny person out from inside of you. Some Mums arrive with their carefully handwritten birth plan and a list of requests extending from specifically scented candles to particular songs. Nine times out of ten this gets thrown out of the window when things start to get heated, women who deemed it less womanly to accept an epidural are sometimes the one begging for it. Other ladies arrive demanding one then find they fly through the entire experience without it.

There was a Prima I'll never forget, a Polish Yoga instructor who arrived with a cerise pink yoga mat tucked neatly under her right arm, her dreadlocks secured in a ponytail on top of her head. When I asked her if she had considered the options for pain relief she laughed in my face and advised me she was going to breathe her way through labour. At the time I offered her a tight lipped smile reminding her that she could change her mind, up to a certain point any way.

I was so sure she would be one of the ones that would wilt at the first sign of pain but in fairness, to my utmost amazement, she did actually breathe her way through fourteen hours of first time labour. Credit where it is due, the mental strength of that particular woman was unparalleled.

Since qualifying as a midwife I have so much more respect for all of the women I have ever known. Where I come from its normal for women to have ten, twelve or even thirteen children. How they did it was beyond me. It's true what they say, each delivery generally gets easier (providing there are no major complications). But what the body goes through can be barbaric, it hadn't inspired any mothering instinct in me so far anyway.

That day I was working the same shift as Steph again, our friend and colleague who we regularly socialised with. She'd been in the academic year behind us but had opted to stay on post qualification as well. One of my favourite midwifes, Julie, was working with us today. She was about forty eighty and very maternal herself, looking after all of us younger ones. We called her Mamma J. She was a wonderful woman, approachable and kind with a soft Scottish lull and a heart of gold. Her experience had proved invaluable to us as we started fresh faced into this career that was so demanding and ultimately weighted with responsibility.

When I first qualified it used to terrify me that I was the one that was supposed to know what I was doing. It was such a huge undertaking working in a fast paced, unpredictable environment where we were not only responsible for one life, but two. As student's, there was always someone senior to go to for help, in the real world, often you were the only one available until the Obstetrician you paged arrived.Sometimes if he was delivering another baby you had to be confident enough to make some difficult decisions.

'Hi Julie.' I waved at her across the clinic, delighted to be on the same shift again.

'Orla. How are you darling?' She looked up from whichever chart she was examining, Pauline would have probably had a word in her ear by now.

As lovely as she was, she could be equally terrifying should you cross her, not that I ever had. Nor did I intend to. She had a son, James, who she clearly adored and despaired of at the same time. He had dropped out of medical school two years into his degree, then after her husband had persuaded him to go and study Dentistry he stuck at that for six months before he quit to travel the world. He had been back for a couple of months now and still didn't know what he wanted to do with his life so he was back at home with Mamma J. She gave off holy hell about him, but she clearly loved every single hair on his head.

'Three in the waiting room.' Julie nods towards the tiny room just outside the door to Labour Ward.A leather sofa occupies the back wall on the far side of the waiting room; leather was the only job for leaking waters (sorry, too much information?). Smaller green leather chairs lined the opposing wall. A large, tattered selection of magazines occupied the wooden shelves, I doubt they'd ever been read, they must have come in tatty because the last thing women in labour want to do is read a magazine.

'Have we got a room for them yet?' I ask Julie as she finished taking the handover from the graveyard nurses, two of whom were still stuck in private rooms with women they had been attending to all night and four who had just left the ward for the locker room.

'Laura is just prepping room five and Anna is organizing seven.'

'Great. Where do you want me?'

'Go to room two, here are the notes, Jessica will fill you in. Last time I checked Mum in two was seven centimetres dilated so hopefully we will have some movement soon. Dr Sanderson is still here, he'll be in to examine her before he does his handover with Dr Crawford.' It was funny hearing Simon spoken about so formally at work when I'd heard the other extreme from my best friend's overly descriptive accounts of their not so private, private lives!

I nodded, took the notes and knocked quietly before entering the small ten by twelve foot room. Jessica looked delighted to see me; mascara lined her eyes as though she'd been at a nightclub, her lank hair greasy and tired. The cavalry at last had arrived. It looked like it had been a long night. I introduced myself to Mum and Dad, shaking their hands and Jessica briefed me on the situation.

Mum had been given Pethidine about an hour ago, she had been doing extremely well, wanted to avoid an epidural if possible (why was beyond me but I kept my opinion to myself). The contractions had been getting closer and more intense the last hour or so without any further dilation. She decided to take the relief now before the real work started, 'The Push'. Just when you feel like you've got nothing left to give, you have to dig deeper than ever before and find it in you to sprint the last mile of the marathon, bare feet with your fanny on fire! That was how one mother described it to me a few years ago and it had stuck with me ever since.

'How are you?' Jessica asked.

'Great.' She didn't need to know about my upcoming weekend,

it would take too long to explain. Apart from the fact we had a patient dozing off three foot away from us and Jessica was undoubtedly desperate to escape to the comfort of her warm bed, we didn't really have that kind of relationship.

I had to try and keep some level of professionalism here, to not just spill my guts to anyone that was willing to listen. Work was the best kind of distraction for me at the minute. I didn't have the luxury of having my head anywhere else but in the game. The initial shock having worn off, I was far more able to concentrate than I had been only a couple of short days ago. Jessica left and I addressed Mum and Dad, trying to get the measure of them before things really got started in here. Dad perched on the edge of his wife's bed while she drifted off, a delightful side effect of the Pethidine.

I smiled at him reassuringly. His nose was a little red and his shirt pulled tightly over his pot belly revealing small patches of hairy white flesh. If I was a betting woman, I'd put money on the fact that this man liked a drink. I could spot it a mile away after my upbringing. But he was very attentive to his wife, looking nervous as most men in here do, unsure of what horrors they may be about to witness before they get their hands on that sweet, long awaited prize.

'Do you know if it's a boy or a girl?' I asked him, initiating conversation in the hope of putting him at ease.

'No. Sandy didn't want to find out.' He tells me, only taking his eyes off of her momentarily.

'A surprise is lovely.' I tell him as I start recording Sandy's observations.

'To be honest we don't want to count our chickens.' He said solemnly.

'Ah I know, I think everyone feels like that to some extent.' I try to reassure him.

'We've had a few miscarriages.' He explains.

'Ah. God love you. It's an awful thing to go through.'

'Seven of them.' He said.

'Jeez, that's absolutely horrific I am so sorry to hear that.' And I truly meant it. Heartfelt sorry. Everyone has their own problems. Mammy always said if everybody were to put their troubles outside into the middle of the street, at the end of the day you would always take back your own, there were always people so much worse off.

'Then there was the ectopic pregnancy. That nearly broke her.' He continued, nodding at Sandy as she turned her head to the other side trying to support her neck. Sleeping half upright was no mean feat.

'I am so sorry. Please God you will get your happy ending in a few short hours now. She's in great hands here.' I silently sent up a prayer that this would be the day it all worked out for them. But there were no guarantees for anything in this life. I crossed my fingers behind my back and offered him some tea while he had the chance. He gratefully accepted.

Unusually the Midwifery Assistants appeared to be doing the dreaded stock take, a job we all avoided like the plague. I suppose we did only have three women in at the minute, the earlier rush of the morning seemingly dealt with. Dare I even think the Q word?In really awful times we'd actually had women on trolleys in the corridor giving birth, though that was not something we advertised.

There were gas cylinders, masks, leads, paper rolls, ultrasound gels, boxes of gloves, paper charts and God knows what else scattered all over the ward. It baffled me that they were undertaking this job right now. Curiosity got the better of me.

'Have they nothing better to be at?' I asked Steph.

'You know that guy that we saw in the Canteen on Monday? The good looking one with the dark hair?' She replied.

How could I forget him? I'd barely been able to stop thinking about him since our encounter in the hall yesterday. I nodded slowly, hoping it wasn't written all over my face. I looked away casually to mask my sudden questionable interest.

'His name is Tom. He works for the Nationwide Funding Department or something. He's demanding to know how much money's worth of stock we've got in that cupboard. The girls are moaning because he was right when he said it hadn't been done properly in forever. There were antibiotics in the back of the fridge that passed their sell by date three years ago!' Steph shrugged her shoulders, she was a stickler for doing things by the book so this type of organisation would come as a welcome relief to her.

The harsh clicking of heels on the lino floor alerted us to the arrival of one of the grey haired receptionists from the front desk on the ground floor, the noise echoed off the hospital walls, bouncing along the corridor. She approached us brandishing a massive bouquet of red roses complete with an enormous crimson bow wrapped around the stems, clearly looking for the recipient. Flowers weren't unheard of in the Labour Ward but we didn't encourage them due to the MRSA associated risks.

My face dropped as she headed straight towards me with a clipped smile on her face. She planted the beautiful bouquet on the work surface we share in the corridor to exchange notes.

'For you!' She announced handing me the delivery card.

'Got a new boyfriend have you love?' The admin staff were always after a bit of gossip.

'They can't be for me, must be a mix up.' I protest trying to push them back towards her as she raised her hands up to push them straight back at me. This sort of thing never happened to me. My mouth was wide open in horror, embarrassed at her mistake.

'They must be meant for someone else. Maybe one of the Mums?'

'No. It looks like you've caught somebody's eye, they've got your name on them hen! Look, Orla Broder, 3rd Floor, Labour Ward.'

I looked at the tiny envelope in my hand and ran my fingers over the back of it. It wasn't the first envelope I'd opened this week with uncertainty. The receptionist stood tapping her feet in anticipation, blatantly waiting for some news to report back downstairs. I pulled out the rectangular white card and a blush of colour rose guiltily up my cheeks, a tell-tale crimson flush.

'Dinner tonight 8pm? T x'

Tom, as he was apparently called, picked that precise moment to walk through the narrow corridor with a mountain of green paper files in his strong arms and wink at me meaningfully. His paced slowed to a deliberate crawl, the question apparent in his uncertain gaze. For a brief unmistakable second he looked momentarily nervous as he awaited my response.

The thought of spending time alone with him was powerfully enticing, despite my initial reservations, I had the distinct impression it was only a matter of time before I would cave anyway. For a split second I stood transfixed on the flowers, a little shocked, yet fully aware there could only be one answer. Brazen was his approach, especially after I'd rebuffed his initial interest. I admired that he was persistent. I dared myself to give it a go, it was only dinner. A slow smile spread across my face in defeat as I succumbed, inevitably. This was probably not a good idea but my instincts compelled me to give it a chance. I reminded myself he was leaving in a few short weeks anyway, what's the worst that could happen?

I nodded briefly at him across the clinic answering his unspoken question and he winked again, returned the nod and quickened his pace before anybody could notice our rapid exchange.

The receptionist turned round to crane her neck to see who I was nodding at but he was long gone. 'Well?' She asked impatiently.

'Secret admirer apparently.' I lied as I stuffed the card back into the envelope, tucking it into my scrub pocket for safe keeping.

'Huh.' The receptionist was unimpressed, desperate to be the one to deliver any snippet of juicy gossip back to her colleagues and fellow cronies back on the front desk. She turned on her heels, dusted imaginary dirt from her mustard patterned blouse and stalked away, heels clicking furiously on the floor again.

I turned back towards the shared computer and Steph raised her eyebrows suggestively at me, clocking the entire brief but meaningful exchange with Tom. Whoops.

'Mums the word.' She said wiggling her eyebrows up and down. I trusted her.

Mum and Dad in Two delivered a healthy baby boy weighing a grand total of seven pounds and three ounces almost two hours later. I cried with them as Dr Crawford handed them their beautiful baby boy stark naked, covered in mucous, to be placed on Mum for the essential skin time. It was an absolute miracle for them and it made my week to be a part of it.

Before my shift ended at seven pm I had another lady prepped and ready for theatre, she was going for a C-section following zero progress over a ten hour period. I was grateful to be finished but also hated leaving the Mums I'd spent the day with, especially when they were close to the end. If I didn't leave the building now I would never get out of there.

As far as Friday the thirteenths had gone, it had been relatively uneventful, apart from the obvious flowers, although that nights date was yet to come. At least I didn't have long to stress about it, possibly the best way.

I changed quickly, throwing my blood splattered scrubs into the laundry basket. Hospital policy dictated they were washed centrally for cross infection control I grabbed my bag, fumbled for my car keys and collected my embarrassingly large bouquet of roses before heading down in the lift and out the back door through the hospital car park into the fresh November air. My Z4 was parked in the staff allocated area which was thankfully well lit. There had been a few unsavoury incidents in the last couple of years which had led to the installation of new lighting and CCTV, providing us nurses and midwives a small modicum of comfort as we finished our shifts and wandered out into the darkness of the night.

As I drove home on auto pilot I mentally flicked through my wardrobe trying to decide what would be deemed suitable for tonight's last minute date, unsure of where we were going. It wasn't an easy task, but I concentrated intently on tonight, it offered the perfect distraction, pushing any thoughts of tomorrow as far out of my mind as possible. An involuntary shiver traced the length of my spine thinking about it. All the worrying in the world wouldn't help. After years of no contact, it had waited this long, I was damn sure I was going to try not to worry about it tonight.

Tom's dinner offer was probably the only thing that could successfully distract me from the dread of what tomorrow might bring, there was no way I was going to turn that opportunity down. That and the fact that he sparked more interest in me than any other man I'd encountered in the last ten years. Behind the bolshie exterior, in the short time I'd spent with him, he'd already revealed an unexpected depth to him, maybe it was the couple of years he undoubtedly had on me. I couldn't help but wonder what other hidden layers he may be concealing. And those enormous blue eyes and his chiselled features were some of the things I was looking forward to examining more closely over dinner.

I used the only coping mechanism I could implement, mentally creating an image of a cardboard box, one that we used to pack up the few belongings I'd owned when I moved to Edinburgh all those years ago. I watched myself squash my worries about tomorrow into it. In my vision, I taped the box tightly closed using industrial strength black masking tape, double wrapping it just to make sure. Satisfied for now I imagined myself sitting on the box as I turned the radio on to accompany me the short drive home.

I'd managed to successfully get lost in the days work, managed to temporarily forget everything else. Mindfulness they called it. It felt like mindlessness to me, but whatever worked. I let myself into the apartment, flung the car keys down onto the kitchen work surface and flicked on the kettle for a cup of tea.I kicked my shoes off into the cupboard and paced the lounge, rearranging the flowers, trying to find a suitable spot for them while I waited for the low hissing of the kettle to begin.

There was some kind of commotion outside my living room window which wasn't unusual for Lothian Road to be honest. It was a great central location in the heart of the City and although it was starting to get revamped and renovated, it housed all sorts.

I crossed the length of the room to peer out of the window. A young girl in her early twenties lay on the pavement wearing only a short, satin nightdress. She was pounding her fists on the slabs, wailing and crying. It wasn't exactly a surprise, unfortunately I'd witnessed this scenario before. A woman in her forties, a business type sporting a suit, crouched down next to her in an attempt to help. It was unusual in the city for people to get involved in others problems, most chose to look the other way, unlike my hometown Kinvarra. Not this woman though, unfortunately for her. I'd seen it all before. This particular young girl may look like a tortured angel crying in her cream attire, but she had the voice of the devil. She began to hurl a constant stream of obscenities at the woman who looked completely startled and took a few steps back in surprise. Time to intervene.

I didn't bother putting my shoes back on, leaving the door on the latch and ran up the next flight of steps onto the fourth floor. Chapping the panel of the second door I came to, an elderly lady answered. She peered out the side of the door that was only ajar about four inches, her grey hair curled up in rollers on each side of her head.

'Mrs Evans, I'm afraid your daughter is out on the street causing a hell of a commotion again. She must be freezing, she's only in her night dress!'

'Oh no, Orla I thought she was in her room, that God awful music's still blaring out from in there. Load of old racket it is hen! You know I don't let her watch the television, she's daft enough as it is.' I could hear Nirvana's 'In Utero' emerging from the corridor behind Mrs Evans.

'Want me to help you fetch her?' I'd seen Mrs Evans with her unstable daughter a few times but never actually spoke to the girl myself, the only reason I knew my elderly neighbour is because I'd taken in parcels for her when she wasn't home.

'No doll, you're okay, thanks for letting me know. I bet she's been making herself sick to bring back up the medication. She's sure she's being poisoned the poor love. She thinks it's a conspiracy theory. I try to remind her that I'm her Mother but she just stares at me with this vacant look on her face. Thanks for letting me know.' She turns to get her coat and keys.

I thought my problems were bad. It kind of puts it in perspective for you when you see other people have just as many problems as you do, some even worse. I head back to the flat to find that my kettle still hasn't boiled. On closer examination I notice it's unplugged at the wall. I take it as a sign and pour myself a small glass of chilled Pinot Grigio from the fridge to sip on while I get ready.

Hard to believe I have a date with The Dub, it happened so quickly, which is probably why I agreed. I didn't have time to over analyse and think of a million reasons why I should have said no. Life is ironic the way it throws everything at you at once, the arrival of two men in my normally simple life, albeit different circumstances. Perhaps it's easier to deal with this way, rather than obsessing over just one thing at a time. Confronting multiple situations, maybe everything will find a more balanced perspective. Or maybe I'd have a complete melt down, shut the front door and hide under the duvet until everything goes back to normal. Not that it could.

I peeped out of the window; the commotion seeming to have died down for now. Sending a quick text to Samantha, I inform her of the last minute date, knowing full well she will be over the moon. I just have one more job to do before I can get ready, ring Mammy; she answers with the usual greeting.

'867922'

'Hi Mammy.'

'Orla! I've been thinking about you all day. Are you ready for tomorrow?'

'I'm anxious. Trying not to think about it.' I bite my lower lip as the apprehension spreads like wildfire from my core to my limbs.

'Listen to me my girl and listen hard. You walk in there tomorrow, head held high. Let him do the talking. He asked to see you not the other way round.'

'Thanks Mam.' Just the reassuring tone of her voice made me feel better.

'Just be prepared sweetheart, it won't be pretty, you know yourself what chemotherapy does to you. At least Jack will be there with you, you'll feel better once it's done.'

'Thanks Mam I know, it's just the thought of it. After all these years it's hard enough, let alone now he's ill.'

'I'm so proud of you Orla. It might sound silly but I think you're doing the right thing.After all, you owe him nothing. It just shows what a lovely woman you've grown in to.' She was getting all sentimental on me, I had to wonder if she'd had a glass of wine herself already this evening. Breda seemed to be becoming increasingly emotional as the years passed. She's had some hard years in her life. No wonder she didn't want to see Daddy.

'Thanks Mam, for everything. You've always been so supportive of me whatever decisions I made. I love you.'

'And I love you. Now let's stop all of this mushy stuff before you make your old Ma cry! I'll have the dinner ready for you tomorrow night.' Food was Breda's answer to every problem life threw at us.

'Well I suppose there is some other news...' I begin to tell her.

'Tell me!' Now I have her attention.

'I was asked out on a date tonight and I accepted.' I inform her, delighted to be able to talk about anything other than tomorrow.

'With who? One of them men in skirts?' She asks tutting.

'No. A guy from work. He's actually Irish.' I reply, knowing full well this little snippet of information will please her.

'Ooh. Is he a Doctor?' What is it that is so prestigious about being married to a Doctor? Surely if you wanted that kind of prestige you would just become a Doctor yourself?

'No Mammy, he's a Contractor. I barely know him yet and I'm not sure how long he will be around for. But tonight of all nights, I could be doing with taking my mind off of things with a bit of company.' I put it simply.

'Where is he taking you?'

'No idea at all, I assume he's picking me up, he didn't actually say.'

'Does he know where you live?' Poor Breda was genuinely baffled, bewilderment seeped through her tone.

'Mam I've no doubt he would have looked it up on the computer.'

'Orla!' She exclaimed in alarm. 'Don't tell me your address and your contact details are on the bloody internet! You never know who's looking at them, there could be perverts looking or anything! Those paedophiles or stalkers, you name it, they are out there!' Poor Breda was definitely panicking now, never one for technology, she could just about send a text message.

'You're not on one of them dating agencies online are you? Match.com or something? Because that big girl Clare that lives two doors down from the surgery on the other side of the road, she once met a man on the internet!' She rushed into another one of her elaborate stories about one of the village people I barely knew. I sat down on the leather couch and said nothing, fully aware that this could go on for a while, once she got started.

'When she actually met up with him in Galway City he was actually at least twenty years older than his picture! And he weighed about twenty stone! Mind you, I don't know what picture she sent him right enough!'

I could actually hear the panic rising in her voice as she jumped to all sorts of wild conclusions in her head. As usual she spoke so quickly I could barely get a word in edgeways. Intermittently I opened my mouth to unsuccessfully interrupt her, in an attempt to ease her mind, but she continued on without a break. I rolled my eyes to the heavens and waited for my chance to speak.

'And you never know who these people are, they could be murderers, rapists, terrorists, you just wouldn't know! Orla? Orla are you still there?'

I tried to answer but I was shaking with uncontrollable laughter.

'What's so funny? I don't think it's a laughing matter at all, it's really very worrying!'

'Breda! Calm down! I never even mentioned the internet. My details are on the system at work, in his job he has access to all of it. It's just a database Mam for staff eyes only. Calm down, you'll burst a blood vessel or give yourself another grey hair.' I was still chuckling.

'Hmm. You'll know yourself one day when you have your own children. You'll be worried sick about them, trust me. And you'll be left wondering what a megabyte or a gigabyte is! You youngsters live in a different world I'm telling you.' She was chuckling a little herself now.

'Right well I better go. I need to get ready.' I was conscious that eight o'clock was only half an hour away.

'Yes, well enjoy yourself. And be careful!' She couldn't help but add.

'Will do.' I try to reassure her, grateful that she hasn't yet mastered Skype or FaceTime to catch me rolling my eyes.

'See you tomorrow. Safe travelling. Love you, bye, bye, bye, bye, bye, bye.' And with that she was gone. I looked down at the handset in wonder still laughing. She was a ticket.

I shaved my legs, moisturized, plucked, buffed and eventually began to dry my unruly hair, which always takes forever because it's so thick. When I was a child I detested my red hair, separating me from everyone else in our tiny country school. Now I love it, embracing being different. It's unreal how many women comment on the colour with apparent envy. It went from being the bane of my life to becoming an unexpected bonus.

Selecting a simple emerald green dress, cut lowly with satin banding under the bust, I decided less was more and the shade complimented my colouring. I doused myself in Coco Chanel and shoved it into a small clutch for later. Jason Mraz sung lightly in the background from my iPod docking station as I sipped on the glass of chilled white wine. Getting dressed up was half the fun, I barely even recognized myself as the midwife in the scrubs only an hour earlier.

Eventually my hair is straight, my make-up perfectly in position. I apply a deep cherry coloured lipstick to match my nails. Coincidentally the lipstick is Maybelline 18 hour, it does not come off on glasses, lips, collars, or anything else for that matter. So on the off chance I get 'the shift' (as we call it at home), it won't budge. Oil based make remover is the only thing that removes it, whoever invented it deserves an award.

The woman that stared back at me from the full length mirror was a far cry from the girl that left Ireland all those years ago.

She looked far more sophisticated than I ever felt; self-assured, confident and poised. Would Daddy even recognise me? Again, I force myself to picture the box, the masking tape and I sit my full weight on the lid on top for good measure.

Waiting in the lounge I left the music and candles on, enjoying the quiet calm of my apartment after the manic day on the ward. Would he come up or should I go down? It wasn't my style to be standing around waiting for a man.Actually it was previously unheard of. At the granite island in the kitchen I attempted to collect my thoughts for a few minutes. It had been a long time since I met a man than stirred any real interest, yet tonight there was no denying the distinct fluttering of butterflies in my stomach, I wasn't sure I liked it. I definitely didn't trust it. A lot of women are desperate to meet somebody special, fall in love and get married, but for some reason the thought of it never really appealed to me. A therapist would have a field day with me I'm sure, no doubt attributing it to my broken family, but in this day and age broken families were the new norm.

I couldn't decide if the timing of Tom arriving into my life was awful or wonderful, with the situation with Daddy and the complications that went with it. But either way, he wasn't going to be in Edinburgh for long anyway. I didn't know much about him, only that he was leaving in a few weeks. Which is probably one of the reasons he appealed to me, there is no danger of getting tied down. Mentally Iprobably wasn't in the best shape to be dating, but an overpowering gut instinct overrode my apprehension. If I ever needed a distraction in my life it was now. Maybe the timing was actually perfect, for what it would amount to.

The buzzer loudly interrupted my thoughts, I look down at my delicate silver watch, a Christmas present from my brother, eight o'clock on the dot. He's punctual at least. Picking up the intercom I inhale a large mouthful of air and blow it out slowly through my nose like I'd seen so many women do before me on the ward. Buzzing him into the apartment block I watched him approach through the peep hole of my wooden front door. He clutched a bottle of Moet under his left arm, his expression calm and confident. Holding my breath silently I waited for him to knock on the very door that I'd never admit I was standing behind. He does so without a second or hesitation.

Pausing for a few seconds, in a lame effort not to appear as eager as I felt, I opened the door a genuine and broad grin infringed upon my face, any anxiety melted away at the sight of his tanned, warm face and the reassuring twinkle in his eyes.

'Good evening Miss Broder.' He took the liberty of leaning in to kiss me on the cheek as he presented the bottle of bubbly to me. His touch sparked an undeniable self-awareness within me, alerting me to desires that until recently, I hadn't realised I owned. The effect he had on me was absurd, but there was no denying it.

'Call it an ice breaker if you like.' He referred to the champagne.

'Thank you.' I replied.

'I couldn't help but notice the other night in the bar that you had exceptional taste.' He laughed at his own easy innuendo, shrugging his shoulders jovially.

Holding the door open wide for him to enter, he strolled through to the sitting room and brushed slowly past me, his aftershave lingering in the corridor temptingly. I was aware of his every movement. He glanced around the room, nodding approvingly at my home, my private sanctuary. It was cosy, clean and warm, an open plan area, designed for relaxation. After the religious statues and crosses at home in Galway I'd opted for minimalistic and modern décor.

'You really do have great taste.' He informs me again, looking at the enormous cushions, throws and canvas wall art. I'm not convinced it's actually great taste or safety in simplicity, but I didn't correct him. He leant back casually against the breakfast bar, intently eyeing me from head to toe, causing me to feel momentarily shy under his examination.

'You look absolutely stunning.' He concluded, eyes lingering over the dress appreciatively. Again, without the initial bravado, a genuine warmth tinged his every word. Almost as an afterthought he crossed the floor to reach me and held his hand out to shake mine.

'I'm Tom by the way. Tom Rourke.' He smiled that killer smile flashing his straight, evenly set pearly whites at me once again. 'I'm sure you already know that by now, but I suppose it's only polite to introduce myself properly.' His handshake was gentle but strong. The explosive heat from his touch spread rapidly up my forearm like wild fire, tingling through every nerve in my body.

'It's a pleasure to meet you Tom.' My voice was low and sincere, barely more than a whisper. 'Tom, the Dub.' I divulged his private nickname and he laughed.

'Orla, the Galway Girl.' Touché.

'Shall I do the honours then?' He motioned to the bottle sitting on the side.

In the familiarity of my own lounge, with Jason Mraz still singing softly in the background and the scent of Tom's citrusy aftershave teasing my nostrils, I found myself for once, short of words. I was irrefutably attracted to him, but the real draw was the cool confidence that radiated from his every pore, with every gesture. His strong, calm, presence was simply therapy to me, I allowed him to take the lead tonight. This date was his suggestion, his idea. I gave myself to his care, allowing the worries of the week to melt away for tonight at least. Not exactly the events themselves, more the feeling of despair that accompanied them.

In this instance, tonight was all that existed to me; the rest of the world could wait. Whether I planned to give it to him or not, he had secured my undivided attention. This was a better distraction than even I had dared to hope for. Accepting the fact that what would be, would be, I crossed the kitchen, stilettoes clicking on the tiled floor. Lifting out two Swarovski champagne glasses I handed him the bottle to do the honours. I couldn't be trusted not to break a window with the cork. He expertly poured the champagne into the crystal flutes and raising his up, we clinked our glasses together lightly in a toast.

'To us.' He said, the air charged with the electricity of illicit possibilities, which I could only attribute to the simple fact that we were both fully aware of the chemistry between us and the small matter of his imminent departure in a few short weeks. He was here for a good time, not for a long time, of that I was sure. But it suited me down to the ground. I wondered briefly if it meant we could fast forward through all the bullshit of the usual laws of dating, because we both knew that this was not a relationship that was ever going to go anywhere.

I felt an overwhelming physical desire to kiss him, to feel him on me, his skin against mine. An irrational attraction vastly overpowered my usual sensible self. He gazed down into my eyes, more than aware that he was scorching my soul with the intensity of his stare, a knowing glint in his eye mocked me, daring me to do what I so obviously desired, enjoying the effect he was creating, the havoc he was wreaking with my hormones.

He leaned in closer to further test my willpower, mere inches between us, I could feel his breath on my lips.As I closed the gap reaching up onto my tip toes, I could feel my breasts brushing against his chest. Never before had I been so aware of myself until this precise moment, aware of every fibre in my being, every single sensitive cell screamed at me to do something unheard of.

He waited motionlessly, enjoying our intimate proximity, watching the good Catholic sensible old me, internally duelling with the new brazen, self-aware me, not once breaking the stare. Only millimetres between us now, I feared I would physically burst with a longing I hadn't realised I possessed. His scent intoxicated me, pulling me closer still. I pushed myself forward closing the final space, the devil inside me won, celebrating her victory by pressing my hips shamelessly against his. Without further hesitation his warm, full lips came crashing down on me, his tongue pushed and thrusted back and forth, dancing illicitly with mine.

Lifting me effortlessly like a doll onto the cold granite work surface, his fingers gently traced my back, my waist and hovered close underneath my bust. Placing my hands around his neck, my fingers grasped at his short hair, he nudged forward pushing his hips between my legs. If this was the way the date was beginning, I was fairly sure where it would end. Maybe it was the exact release that I needed.

CHAPTER NINE

—

Saturday 14ᵗʰ November 2015

Another Saturday morning with a dry mouth and a champagne headache, rolling over I hit the snooze button. There was a brief interlude between sub consciousness and reality, several seconds of ignorant bliss before the reality of the situation struck, I had a plane to catch. Unfortunately not to Barbados or some other exotic Caribbean resort. My stomach churned threateningly, a combination of adrenaline and last night's drinks. Merely prolonging the inevitable, hiding under the warm security of the heavy duvet, I allow myself a few moments of reflection before facing the difficult day ahead.

A small smile crept onto my face as I remembered the night before. We didn't make it past the front door in the end, which was unsurprising considering the manner in which the date began. Having missed the dinner reservation at The Tower, we finished the champagne and everything else that was started. Tom certainly appeared to be the full package, excuse the pun. His dry sense of humour matched my own and I found once I relaxed into the evening I enjoyed his company and his body far more than I imagined possible.

His tales of his inner city Dublin upbringing had me laughing and crying at points as he described how he was the youngest of eight siblings, a surprise to his forty six year old Mam, even more of a surprise to his siblings as their father had passed away years before. His easy manner and the fact he didn't take himself too seriously put me at ease from the beginning. He was different to how I thought he'd be, absent of the bravado. With the mask dropped, stripped back to the next layer (in every sense) his honesty was enthralling and refreshing. He was much more genuine than I had initially assumed. Because he was so obviously handsome, I'd assumed he'd know it, but there was a flash of vulnerability as he talked about his family and his upbringing. My interest in him only piqued with his unexpected revelations. The good looking God I'd pegged him as showed me that he was in fact only human, and a fabulous one at that.

Hunger crept up on us at about eleven o'clock. I took the liberty of ordering a Chinese which was delivered straight to my door. We had a midnight feast at the high leather stools of the same island he'd devoured me on only a short while earlier. The thunderous cracking of fireworks from the castle alerted us to a nearby wedding party celebrating their newly founded commitment. The exotic display of purple light drew us closer to look out of the lounge sash window. Tom stood behind me, an arm draped lightly round my waist as internal fireworks rocketed through my blood and I found myself searching for his kiss again.

It was amazing the difference one week could make, how life could take an unexpected twist of fate, an unpredictable change in direction without any prior warning. Reluctantly accepting that I wouldn't get any answers from my bed, I showered, washing the faint remaining traces of Tom away, watching as the frothy foamy suds swirled and disappeared down the plughole. The delicious scent of his aftershave lingered on my skin no more. Although my behaviour had been completely out of character, I had no regrets about the way the night progressed. We were both adults who had enjoyed ourselves and I trusted his discretion. I wouldn't normally dream of sleeping with a guy on a first date, but the attraction had been heightening across the clinic unbearably and I was acutely aware that he would soon be gone, moving onto the next hospital and maybe the next nurse.

An irrational stabbing sensation overcame me as an image of

him in his next position flashed through my mind. I swallowed it down and forced myself to get a grip. It's not like I wanted to marry him! Or anyone for that matter. That was always Samantha's dream, not mine.

I remind myself I'm in no fit place for a relationship right now and even if I was, Tom is only here for a few more weeks so he wouldn't exactly be a prime candidate anyway. I'd shocked myself with the way I had literally given myself over to him and so quickly. It had felt so good to let someone else take the reins for a change. The nature in which I was so physically attracted to him made me weak, it was foreign to anything I'd experienced before. If that's the kind of crazy behaviour he inspired, it was a good job he was only going to be around for a few weeks.

We talked about everything and anything, football - a massive thing for us Irish, I'm not talking about that God awful soccer where men break a nail and demand a penalty. I mean Gaelic, the real football that runs through us and in us, the loyalty that is bred into us within our Counties. The fact that he's a Dub would have been a minus point for him in my eyes if we were currently living in Ireland, but here it was a bonus, our shared heritage. Plus he wasn't one of those 'men in skirts' as Mammy called them.

Even after his revelation regarding his unknown father, I neglected to tell him my current situation, the upcoming reunion with my own father. It was too deep for me to fathom and a first date wasn't the time or place. I was still mentally sitting on the cardboard box in my feeble attempt to compartmentalise. Tom was my distraction, and by God what a distraction he had provided.

Offering his undivided attention, he listened intently to my every word, possessing an ability that allowed me to feel as though I was the most interesting woman in the world, though in the light of day I was fully aware that it was far from the truth. Abilities such as those have gotten far less sensible women into deeper trouble! The bottom line after last night was, in addition to being outrageously good looking, he was quick, funny and a gentleman too. Well, most of the time.

I'm fairly sure he would have spent the night in my bed without much encouragement but I drew the line at that. Waking up next to a person is a whole new level of personal, despite the activities of earlier in the evening. I was also fully aware of what today had in store for me, or as aware as I could be. In reality, I had no idea exactly how the events of the day would pan out. It was essential that this morning, my family was the priority. I'd buried my head long enough, it was time to face the music, although the beat, rhythm and lyrics so far escaped me.

Pulling on a pair of navy jeans, a white fitted shirt and chocolate knee length leather boots, I get ready carefully, adamant to look my best, silly though it may sound. I repeatedly reminded myself that I shouldn't care what he thought. He hadn't been there to voice an opinion earlier on in my life, so he certainly didn't deserve one now. But in reality I did of course care, wanting him to be proud of the woman I've grown into. It's irrational that I was still seeking his approval now, but I couldn't help it. Even after years of telling myself I didn't care, didn't need him or any man for that matter, I'd been let down too many times before. I'd need to be careful I wasn't setting myself up for a fall.

Applying a tinted Vaseline to my rosy lips it occurred to me that I couldn't actually recall the last time I saw him, couldn't pinpoint it to one specific memory. There were many days I could clearly remember thinking I'd see him, willing him to arrive, better late than never, but it was wrecking my head trying to conjure up an image of him specific to the last time.

I wheeled my battered travel case out the front door, pulled on a leather jacket, glanced longingly over my shoulder at the safety and comfort of my own home before slamming the door shut, accepting my fate. I made my way down the steps two at a time onto Lothian Road to flag one of the many passing black cabs. It took less than thirty seconds to hail one, traffic was always chaotic here. When I first arrived in the City I used to hear every single engine, every horn, everything. After years of listening to it, I'm immune to all of it.

'To the airport please.' I told the driver. He glanced back at me in the rear view mirror. I made no eye contact and prayed he wouldn't ask me if I was going somewhere nice. I pulled out the phone and pretended to be engrossed in it. As it happened there were two missed calls from Samantha and a text wishing me luck. Breda left a message instructing me to call her when I land safely and Rebecca text to say she was thinking of me.

Edinburgh was overcast, without even a hint of the autumn sun and it suited my sombre mood. Looking up at the grey dreary sky through the taxi window, I tapped my fingers on my bag, drumming to myself as yet another distraction. It wasn't as cold as it has been earlier in the week, the taxi felt stuffy and I let the window down a crack in order to enjoy the familiar sounds and smells of city life. Everybody seemed to be going about their daily business, I only wished I was doing the same.

Outside the airport I handed the driver a twenty and told him to keep the change, grateful for his silence. The Aer Lingus desk was already open, the green uniforms and logo caught my eye immediately. A low hum of conversation and laughter filled the air, loved up couples prepared for romantic holidays, friends gathered togetherreunited or to bid farewell. A group of lads stood in line for the Easy Jet desk to check in for a flight to Amsterdam on a stag do, one guy dressed as a woman and not a particularly attractive one at that. I laughed out loud, once again momentarily forgetting the reason for witnessing all of this chaos.

Two of the guys from the stag party stared at me and whistled as I sauntered past. 'Nice boots!' One of them shouted. I shook my head slightly and smiled brightly, flashing them my straight white teeth, a testament to years of orthodontics in my early twenties.

I took the escalator to Costa Coffee in search of a hot cup of tea, unable to stomach any food. A nervous energy flowed through my veins, jittery in anticipation. Sitting in the burgundy coloured scheme that represents every Costa in the world, I blew on my scalding tea and mulled things over for the millionth time, trying to imagine the worst possible outcome, and then the best. There could be no positive outcome today, whichever way you looked at it.

'This is a final boarding call for Miss Orla Broder please report directly to boarding gate two immediately' A voice announced over the speaker. Shite! I abandoned my tea and ran as quickly as my four inch heels would carry me to the departure gate three hundred metres away. Handing over my boarding card I apologised profusely, engrossed in my own world.

I rushed to find seat 5a and pushed my bag under the one in front, not wishing to hold the plane up any longer. I flopped down next to a dark haired man in his forties who appeared as though he'd won the lottery when he realised I was allocated the seat next to him. Great. Not.

'Hi there.' He said looking me up and down. I nodded hello to him without smiling and put my headphones in. The plane soared through the air and I figured I had about an hour to myself before I had to confront the pain of the past.

Jack was waiting for me in the arrival's area of Knock. It was a small airport but very well serviced, without it I'd have been lost, forced to make the long journey from Dublin. Sensing my arrival he glanced up from his phone and broke into an almighty grin. He crossed the floor to meet me and took my bag for me. I strode towards him as fast as my heels would allow, delighted to see my only brother, embracing him in a big bear hug. He squeezed me back tightly.

'How are you doing, short stuff?' he says, despite the fact I'm actually five foot eight. Tall for a girl, just significantly shorter than him.

'Nervous. Help me get this over with and get me to Mammy's, please.' I pleaded.

'I know. It will be okay, I won't leave you.' He assured me.

'What kind of state is he in?' I asked, unsure if I was ready to hear it.

Jack hesitated, considering his words carefully, attempting to muster a suitable yet honest answer. He placed his arm lightly on my back, gently guiding me through the airport towards the parking lot, the Barcelona flight had just landed and the airport was busier than normal.

'It's terminal. He isn't going to get better. No more options for treatment. His hair is gone. He's lost a ton of weight.'

I said nothing. It was only what I'd expected.

'He's weak, frail and old looking. Emotionally he's all over the show, up and down. Angry and frustrated. I suppose we can't imagine what it feels like, knowing that this is the end.'

I nodded again like a mute, once again short of words for the second time in twenty four hours. Sliding into the Golf GTI I switched on the radio. Today FM were discussing the football results. I turned it off abruptly as it felt inappropriate. Jack negotiated the car out of the parking lot, slotted the ticket back into the meter, the barrier opened and we set off for Galway City, a journey which normally took an hour and twenty minutes depending on traffic.

'What did he say about me?' I wondered if he thought I should have tried harder to find him, to make contact with him. Then I remembered Samantha's words, it was me that was the child, he was the adult. It had been up to him to try to maintain a relationship if that's what he wanted. But it didn't erase the tiny sliver of guilt snaking through the pit of my stomach.

'He wants to make amends. He expects nothing from you. I think he's hoping you might see a different side to him before it's too late, leave you with a better memory.'

The journey was quiet, both lost in our thoughts. Upon reaching our destination, Jack found a parking space in the busy car park and we walked slowly into the hospital building. The overpowering distinctive medical stench slapped me in the face like a wet fish,

72

you'd think I'd be used to that hospital smell given my occupation. They must use a different cleaning detergent to us, it smelt like death, covered partially with the scent of bitter body odour and inadequate amounts of air freshener.

Jack led me through the endless faces of visitors and staff towards the lift to the fourth floor, the signs stating Oncology. It struck me what a horrible word it was, even the way it was pronounced. Tiny fine hairs prickled at the back of my neck, my head felt foggy and each and every limb suddenly seemed to weigh a tonne. The metal doors slid sideways allowing our exit but my boots seemed to adhere to the sticky speckled lino. Jack offered his arm. I took it gratefully, not trusting the direction of my fight or flight reactions as adrenaline fuelled my erratic heart.

We walked slowly to the end of the corridor, the green mile of the building as it were. Daddy's door was the last on the left, slightly ajar in order for the nurses at their nearby station to keep an eye on him. At least he had his own room, however awful this was, it would be a trillion times harder on a ward with an audience.

Jack pushed the door open, entering first with me at his heels, frightened of having my human safety blanket more than a foot away from me. The slow creaking noise of a joint that needed oiling alerted the occupant to our arrival. There a figure lay sprawled out in the bed underneath the window, his head snapping up in silent expectation, his body covered almost entirely with the standard hospital issue bedding. I stared motionlessly at him for what felt like an eternity. My Daddy. The word that had meant the world to me as a young girl, but in reality had amounted to so little.

He was a shadow of his former self, weak, sickly, frail and decrepit. His hair was absent bar a few strange tufts of soft grey strands, eyebrows missing from his face and a few odd clumps of stubble littered the space where his beard used to be. From the outline that I could make out, I ascertained that he couldn't weigh more than seven stone.

The white starched sheets were tucked tightly up over his chest, his thin arms wasting, held close to his sides. His hand clenched in a feeble fist, housing drips that hung from an industrial steel stand, arching intrusively over the bed. Tubes passed from his nose, drips fed into both his arms, his sunken features were a pale shade of ashen grey. His skin sagged lifelessly underneath his steely blue eyes.

I thought I was prepared, as much as I could be anyway.

It turned out that I wasn't.

Initially he appeared angry, put out, furious with the world, or maybe with me. I couldn't be sure. As I took in his condition, he scrutinised me equally as intensely, sizing me up, glaring eyes examining me from my hair to my brown leather boots. His lip curled slightly on one side as he gradually decided he approved of what he saw. Slowly his expression softened over a painstaking few seconds, for which I held my breath unintentionally. His eyes welled slightly.

He had aged unbelievably. He could have passed for seventy or even eighty. The years hadn't been kind to him, or more likely he hadn't been kind to himself. This I was not prepared for. Daddy had always been so strong, ferociously so at times. He had the fighting spirit of a lion, Mammy used to say he'd fight with his own shadow when the mood would take him. Here he was, deflated and beaten.

A single tear rolled from his right eye, trickling the length of his sunken face and he lifted his right arm up cautiously, inviting me to come closer. His wrinkled hand visibly trembled with the fear of rejection. The intensity of his stare bore into me from across the room, questioningly at first, two rabbits caught in separate headlights, both of us unsure which way to turn.

How could I reject him like this? In this state, a shadow of the man he had previously been. The man that lay in front of me now was a different man to the one I had cowered from as a child. He was desperate, at his final hurdle, to make things right. Who was I to deny him peace? Despite the troubles from our past, the wasted years, the missing pieces of our lives and all that had happened before, I was here for a reason. None of that mattered now.

The silent dialogue we exchanged in that single moment covered more than a thousand words. Intense and irrefutable emotion flowed freely between us, crackling and electric in the stifling hospital air. Understanding wove silently and swiftly through the room from him to me and radiated back again. It flooded us, overwhelmingly so.

I'm sorry.

It doesn't matter.

Is it too late?

Do you care?

Of course I care. I've always cared.

Can you forgive me when I can't even forgive myself?

Of course I forgive you.

I love you.

Crossing the room at a rapid rate, the fear that previously haunted me evaporated, I perched on the side of the bed, sitting carefully, afraid of accidentally hurting him. I took his dry rough hand in both of mine and held it, gently looking down at him. I needed to be closer to him, acutely aware of the lack of time we had left, terrified of him withering away in front of me. One thing was certain, he wouldn't hold on much longer, his body was preparing to shut down.

'Hi Daddy.' I murmured quietly. We both understood the significance of that single word. Until this moment I couldn't fully comprehend how much I actually had cared, how the gaping hole that ached in my heart sometimes could never be filled.

As much as I loved Patrick and as much of an amazing father figure he had become over the last twelve years, never would I take his hand and stroke it. With my step father there would always be an invisible line which neither of us crossed, forever aware of that slight awkwardness, we weren't blood. There were no such boundaries today, this was my father.

'Orla. I'm so glad you came. I'm so sorry...for everything.' He hesitated, pausing for breath gathering some modicum of composure before attempting to continue.

'Don't.' I cut him off, there's no point in going over it now. It was done. We had come out the other side. I didn't want to punish him further, he was clearly suffering enough. All that was left was to appreciate the here and now, whatever time we had left. I wanted to get to know my father without a drink in him. To see the man that Breda fell in love with all those years ago. He opened his mouth again to protest and I raised my hand firmly in a silent stop motion.

'Please, I need to tell you…to explain..' He begged as I shook my head.

'It doesn't matter. I promise. Leave it alone…' I pleaded

'Ok. But you know don't you? Just remember, I'm so sorry sweetheart.'

'You don't need to say anything else it's okay, I understand. It's not important anymore. We are here now.'

I look to my brother standing over us, observing quietly. I motion to him to sit on the pale blue arm chair on the other side of the bed.

'How are you feeling today Dad?' He asks concerned.

'Well I'm still above ground so I suppose that's something.' He tried unsuccessfully to make light of the situation, his voice gravelly and strained. Not once did he take his eyes from me, although he addressed both of us.

'I've had about as much chemo as my body will take. I'm tired all the time. I don't have a lot of fight left in me if I'm honest. For once.' Again, he attempted humour but I couldn't bring myself to laugh. Typical Irish using the only mechanism we know, desperate to brush off the seriousness of the situation we face. The outcome was inevitable.

'I'm tired of feeling so sick. I'm relieved that part is all done with.' He referred to the ghastly side effects associated with cancer treatments.

I could barely bring myself to ask the question but I had to know, 'How long do they think?'

'Nobody knows. It could be days or weeks, a couple of months if I'm really lucky. I'm so glad you came.' His sincerity choked me inside, stirring something inside me. I had an overwhelming urge to take care of him, to spend every second with him while I could.

'Well this isn't it, I can stay? Or I can come back next week too if you want?' I can't bear to have found the Daddy that I always wanted him to be then let him go again so quickly.

'Come back tomorrow if you can, or next week.' He smiled a small smile, his tired eyes heavy.

'Have a rest, we'll be right here when you wake up.' I reassured him turning to Jack, 'How about a coffee?'

The afternoon passed all too quickly in the dimly lit room, with Daddy sleeping on and off and chipping into our conversation in between. All of us desperately trying to keep conversation light, steering away from the horrors of the past.

He asked about my job, genuinely interested and proud of my achievements, expressing a degree of surprise that I'd stayed on in Edinburgh. I explained that I missed Mammy obviously, but I had needed to get out while I could, before Kinvarra became all that I'd ever know. I moved on swiftly after that, remembering Breda's request not to talk about her. He seems to sense it and leaves well alone, it's easier all round.

I regale him and Jack with tales of the friends I'd made in Scotland, he laughed as I told him about Rebecca's exploits and

Samantha's initial obsession with the Obstetrician and their upcoming wedding, which she had planned long before their first date.

'And is there a special man in your life that we need to have a chat with anytime soon?' My brother takes it upon himself to ask. An image of Tom's body pressed against mine flashed through my head and the blush threatened to creep into my neck, but I managed to take control it this time.

'Don't be ridiculous!' I scoff. 'Do I look like I'm looking for more work?' I force Tom and everything that happened last night firmly to the back of my mind, it felt like a lifetime ago already.

The nurses came round regularly to administer more drugs and to carry out the standard observational checks on Daddy. They were professional, efficient, friendly but not intrusive. There are no set visiting hours for cancer patients, the hospital respects everyone's needs to make the most of the little time they have left together.

At five o'clock a blonde Australian nurse popped in offering us tea, turning on the lamps as the sun set outside. I sensed she was giving Jack the eye on the sly. Dad appeared to think it was him she was after. Some things never change. My stomach rumbled loudly, disturbing the quiet. I couldn't eat a thing all day. Hunger was the least of my concerns although a short sense of peace enveloped me for that moment. The immediate anxiety, all the wondering, had passed. Mammy was expecting us but I was reluctant to leave. I noticed Jack checking his gold watch discreetly.

'Look at you with that watch you big feckin' poser!' Daddy joked.

'Hmm. You think I'm a poser, this one here,' he nodded at me, 'drives a convertible, feckin' hairdresser car, so it is!'

'I worked hard for that car. You've got to enjoy it while you're young!' I stick my tongue out at my brother inferring that he's wildly past it already. He could probably drive whatever car he liked on his lawyers salary, not that he'd ever say it. It was one of the things I loved about him. He had done well for himself but he liked the simpler things in life.

'Less of your cheek lady. I'm not that much older than you!'

'Well you two haven't changed a bit.' Dad says. 'You used to fight like cat and dog when you were small.'

I was surprised he remembered and it must have been apparent on my face.

'I remember a lot Orla, you'd be surprised. I know you think I missed your school play when you were the Christmas Fairy, God you must have only been about six at the time. But I was there. Admittedly they wouldn't let me in the front door as I was late and if I'm to be honest I'd had a couple of pints.' He shrugged in acceptance of the fact he'd fucked up, continuing anyway with his story.

'I snuck in through the first year classroom window and watched from the back. I was so proud of you girl. I still am.' His expression sagged, sorrowful again.

I remember the exact day he referred to, it had meant the world to me at the time. I wanted so badly to be the Christmas Fairy, I'd lit a candle at Mass every week while they had decided who would play which character. I never thought I would be picked, especially with my red unruly hair.

Mammy sat in the front row, mouthing every rehearsed line she had painstakingly practised with me for weeks beforehand. The empty chair next to her stuck out wildly in a packed room full of proud parents. Yet he had been there after all.

'Come back tomorrow Orla before you fly. Please.'

'I promise I will. Get some rest.' I said solemnly as I tucked him in gently and patted his hand. 'And leave that poor blonde nurse alone for God's sake!'

Jack and I left quietly, thanking the nurses for their kindness on the way out. Silently I pleaded with them in my mind to keep him alive until I come back again, not just the next day but the next week and every week after that. I'd already decided to come as often as I could for the time that God permitted us. I'd taken the number of the telephone beside Dad's bed and typed it into my mobile phone, grateful to have a direct line to him. I'd left him mine scribbled on the back of an old prescription and urged him to call me any hour of the day or night. We got back into the GTI and set off towards Kinvarra, a forty minute drive.

'You did great.' Jack said, as if it were for anyone's benefit other than my own. Truth was I'd actually enjoyed my time there, I hadn't wanted to leave at all.

'I feel like a weight has been lifted. But that doesn't change the fact we don't know how long we will have him for.' I sigh deeply. Its bitter sweet, I was ecstatic to find him again, but already I had to prepare to lose him again, this time for good.

'You made your peace. You made him a very happy man.' Jack reassured me.

'I'll get there as much as possible. I hated leaving him in there, I wish he could come home with us.' My conflicting emotions confused me, I was happy but sad. Strangely content, but almost addicted to the thought of being with him at the same time.

'You know that's impossible for a hundred reasons. We can't care for him Orla. It's essential he stays where he is.' He patted my knee, both of us deep in thought again throughout the drive.

Neither of us acknowledged that apart from the fact we couldn't take care of him, Breda still didn't want to see him. There was also the tiny matter that she had a new husband. A man who put her back together after Daddy had broken her fragile heart into a thousand fragmented pieces.

A short while later we pulled into the gravel driveway of our childhood home. Mammy still lived in the same stone house she always had, she'd never dream of moving. It was in her blood, this was where she belonged and she was a very house proud woman. She stood in the doorway dressed in a royal blue jumper and navy jeans and flat ankle boots. Her arms opened widely and her smile extended from ear to ear, flashing us her neat little line of worn teeth. It was rare she had both of us home at the same time. Jack was based in Limerick or Dublin for work most of the time.

'Well God Bless the both of you and welcome home. I can't tell you how happy it makes me to see you both here together!' She threw her arms around us, squashing us in an uncomfortable embrace, but we indulged her. Nothing like a trip to the Oncology Ward to provide you with a little more patience for the ones you loved.

'Hi Mammy.' Something about the comfort and security of being home again made me want to cry huge tears of relief, but of course I didn't. As I walked through the front door the familiar smell of home overwhelmed me, a thousand memories simultaneously flooded to the surface, the first one being Mary Murphy on the tiled hall floor ten years ago.

The many years of Christmas's, with Mammy and Daddy and Mammy's brothers sitting round the dinner table, pulling crackers, drinking sherry, laughter filling the air. Everybody smoked back then, it was long before the health implications were revealed. Smoke hung in the air in this house for years, staining the long since replaced wallpaper. Then there was Jack's first Holy Communion, the whole family round again, cake, prayers, punch and party dresses. Daddy asleep in the chair, probably intoxicated but there, nonetheless.

'It's ok Pet, its ok.' Breda told me patting my arm, sensing my frail emotional state. She lead me through to Patrick in the kitchen, pulling out a chair at the big oak dining room table for me to take the weight from my feet.

'How are things?' Jack and Patrick shook hands warmly and he gave me a kiss on the cheek as Breda boiled the kettle for some tea.

'Something smells good Ma.' Jack told Mammy appreciatively, sniffing the air.

'I thought you might be hungry. I've got a roast chicken in the oven. It will be about half an hour or so, I wasn't sure what time to expect you.' She said pulling out mugs and a big steel industrial sized teapot.

Glancing around the familiar kitchen, seeing the Cross on the wall and the portrait of the Pope, I noted that nothing had changed in years. My family weren't any more religious than any other family in Ireland, shrines and statues were normal where we were raised, in this predominantly Catholic country. They stuck out to me today after coming from Edinburgh, a multicultural city where I had no idea who believed in what, including myself now.

It certainly made a person question the concept of God when you see pregnant mothers so close to meeting the love of their life, following months of anticipation, the promise of overwhelming joy just around the corner, to then deliver a stillborn baby. Or a terminally sick baby, who enter the world only to leave it a few short minutes later. In my more subdued moments I found myself wondering what the point was in it all. Life could be so cruel. I tried to shake off the morbid feeling but I was very sombre, tired after everything, emotionally I'd been on a rollercoaster for the last week. Yesterday's late night hadn't helped, although I had enjoyed it immensely.

I tried to enjoy the comfort of being surrounded by my family but all I actually wanted to do was head back to Galway City Hospital. Memories of this house and Daddy pulled me towards him, the threatening ticking of the clock fresh in my mind and in my heart.Picking at my dinner I tried to look as though I was listening but I was exhausted, with nothing left to give, adrenaline supply depleted, running on fumes.

Jack offered to take me out for a drink to our local but I couldn't be bothered, I was shattered. Plus I didn't want to see any of the neighbours and deal with questions about how long I'm home for and did I know such and such. Undoubtedly they would have heard about Daddy. I just wanted to hide for now.

Patrick did the dishes leaving the three of us to enjoy one another's company in the sitting room. I took my boots off and made myself comfortable on the sofa. Flicking through the sky channels, I selected an old rerun of Father Ted.

'Want to talk about it?' Mammy asked gently.

'No Mam. Thanks. Trying to get my head round everything.' I say quietly. She nods and settles next to me on the big comfy couch.

I must have nodded off because I woke up with a thick duvet covering me, the red dot of the standby button on the television alerting me to the fact I was still on the couch. The sound of Jack talking softly in the kitchen filtered through to where I lay in the lounge. He was reassuring Mam that we were both fine.Dad however was not fine, but we knew that already. I closed my eyes again, grateful to fall back into a deep dreamless sleep.

CHAPTER TEN

—

Sunday 15th November 2015

The sofa was surprisingly comfortable, the absence of the anxiety and anticipation had finally allowed me to get a decent nights' sleep. There were two perfectly good bedrooms, one of which was my childhood room but I was dead to the world, oblivious to where I lay my head.

The visit to Dad was shorter this time, he was tired looking, even more so than yesterday if possible, but delighted to see us all the same. I promised to check my shifts and ask for a few extra days off in order to stay a bit longer the next week, determined to make the most of whatever time we had left.Breda was delighted I would be home again so soon. I wondered briefly if she was wavering on her decision to see him one last time. She couldn't meet my eye as she asked about him this morning.

I stayed with Daddy as long as I could but I had a flight to catch.

'Take these.' I set up an audio book on my iPad for him and gave him some headphones.

'What am I meant to do with these yokes?' He frowned at the tiny ear phones, squinting at them suspiciously.

'Take them Daddy you might like to listen to a book. I've downloaded a couple on there for you.' I had a Muhammed Ali story preloaded on it and Alex Ferguson's autobiography. Dad had been a United fan for as long as I could remember.

He insisted he didn't need them but I wanted to leave something of me with him, for comfort and to remind him of my imminent return. The thought of him being lonely here by himself ate me alive. I seriously contemplated offering my resignation in Edinburgh but I had a recently acquired mortgage that needed paying despite the circumstances. Jack advised me not to do anything rash, Daddy could be gone in a week or two. I suggested I phone work and tell them I needed time off, but he reassured me it could be a few weeks either yet, it was the not knowing that was hard.

Seeing my emotional state before I left, Daddy assured me he was planning on sticking around for a while yet. Ever the joker, I managed to muster a small smile but I was sorry to be leaving him. If it were possible my heart felt heavier than on the plane trip only a day earlier, but for an entirely different reason.

Jack dropped me off at the airport again and insisted on coming in with me to check in. We had a quick Americano before I took off.He was great company, solid as a rock and a great source of comfort to me. There were no words, the weekend had been a success, but it didn't take away from the seriousness of the situation. I was devastated that it had taken something like this to bring us back together. As we parted ways until the following weekend, he wrapped his arms tightly around me in a bear hug and made me promise to look after myself.

'Tell that fellow of yours I'm asking for him.' He calls cheekily after me.

'What fellow?' I deny.

'Mam told me, you little ratbag! I want to hear all about it next week. Be good!' He shouted as he left the building.

The flight itself was quick, no luggage to check in or collect which saved hanging around. I arrived back in Edinburgh at three thirty to find Samantha waiting for me in the arrival area.

'What are you doing here?' I was surprised to see her waiting for me all wrapped up in a red coat and a silk black scarf and hat.

'I thought it might be nice to have someone here for you when you landed. You must have had a hard weekend.' She gave me a warm embrace and a kiss on the cheek, linking her arm with mine. The smell of my best friend's perfume reminded me of nights out, cocktails and the fact that I had a separate life here, one without sorrow or any significant complications, after the weirdness of the weekend.

'I can't tell you how much I appreciate it.' I was also exceptionally sure there was an additional reason for her being here. She proved me right as she asked innocently how Friday night went. We made our way out through the automatic doors and into the crisp Edinburgh afternoon. The sky above us darkened menacingly and thunder threatened the grey skies ominously.

'Are you still up for a drink later, maybe some dinner? Daniel's here. Don't worry if you're not up for it he'll totally understand. I told him, I hope you don't mind.' Daniel was Samantha's childhood friend from London. They attended school together in Kensington and spent their teenage years drinking Lambrini in the park when their parents thought they were at a local youth club. I'd often wondered if he was actually in love with her. If he was, she hadn't realised it yet.

'No it's fine, it'll be nice to get out. I could do with a distraction.' As the words fell off my tongue I couldn't help but think of my preferred distraction, but I certainly wasn't going to chase him.

'How was your Dad?' She asked gently.

'Grand, well not grand really, but it went fine. Better than fine if that makes sense?' My brain was exhausted again. I would tell her everything, I always did, but right now I needed some light hearted banter, a little escapism.

'I understand. You can tell me all when you are ready to talk about it. Now Friday night... Tell me everything!' Samantha's eyes glinted mischievously and even I couldn't hide the grin of excitement from my best friend. Reliving Friday night was another way to escape my current family saga. By the time we arrived at the underground car park at my flat in Samantha's red Mini Cooper, I had confessed everything, no detail spared.

'You dirty dog Orla Broder! I swear girl, I didn't think you had it in you!' She looked at me in mock shock.

'Sure, you knew very well it was in me, I'm hardly a virgin!' I replied with a guilty laugh.

'Yeah but you can be a little prudish sometimes!' She teased.

'I am not!' Even as I denied it, I realised there was a hint of truth to her accusation, though I preferred the term private to prudish.

'So have you heard from him since?' She asked.

'Maybe.' I tilted my head to one side, raising my eyebrows for dramatic effect.

'Well don't stop now, you're on a roll!' She informs me.

'He text last night. I replied this morning when I woke up. He wants to take me out for dinner this week.'

'I bet he does! Look what happened the last time he offered to take you out for dinner!' She stifled a giggle. 'When are you going?'

'I'm not sure if I am to be honest.'

'What are you talking about you nutter?' She exclaimed with her cockney twang.

'I've got a lot on my plate right now.' It sounded feeble even to me, though it was true.

'You wanted a distraction! You won't get a better one.' She was right and I knew it but I was still unconvinced.

'I feel bad.' I confessed. 'With everything that's going on at home maybe it's wrong of me?'

She leaned across the car and took my hand. 'Sweetie, what

is going to happen at home is inevitable. I'm sorry to say it, but you know the truth of the matter yourself. Don't deny yourself the chance of finding something that's right for you because of it. Do you think your Dad wants his only daughter to become one of those spinster midwives that we are all terrified of becoming? Want me to go to the shelter now and pick up a few cats for you and maybe some knitting needles on the way home?' She teased.

'You know I don't care about that! It wouldn't bother me if I never met anyone.' That was a blatant lie now. After the events of the weekend I had an inkling I would like to meet somebody one day, someone exactly like Tom.

'Liar!' If your best friend didn't know you were lying, you should be in Vegas.

'Okay, okay.' I held my hands up in resignation, ready to divulge the crux of my concerns.

'I'm not sure there's any point, as gorgeous as he indisputably is, he doesn't live here. He's based in Ireland. Which is probably why I agreed to go out with him in the first place.'

'And? You are Irish aren't you? I would have thought it was a perfect match.'

'I couldn't do the long distance thing, not after Daragh. Look how that turned out. But I would love to see him again.' All of him, if I was brutally honest!

'So do it!' She stated as if it were the simplest thing in the world. Maybe I was over complicating it. He was meant to be a distraction, we were both aware he was only here for a short time. I would try and take it as I had intended, try not to obsess and over analyse it.

'Maybe I will.'

The thought of a repeat of Friday night was exceptionally tempting. If I'd learnt anything from the weekend it was to make the most of every day in life. Tomorrow is promised to none of us.

Maybe I should meet him. He offered to book the Tower again and he promised he would actually take me there this time.

'Are you actually going to get out of the car today Orla?' Samantha startled me, interrupting my thoughts by slamming her driver door closed.

'Sorry!' I got out and rustled in my jacket pocket for the keys.

I decided I would meet him and sent him a quick text suggesting Wednesday before I could talk myself out of it again. As I hauled my travel bag up the stairs, my mobile vibrated in my back pocket. Tom replied instantly with one word, '*Perfect*'.

We got settled in the apartment, Samantha sat at one of the kitchen stools as I searched the cupboards for some biscuits. The kettle whistled noisily as it reached boiling point. It felt so good to be home. Even though Kinvarra is technically home I loved my apartment, loved the fact that it was all mine. I poured the tea into our usual mugs and began to tell Samantha about Daddy. The way he was so physically deflated and emotional. Vulnerable and childlike in a lot of ways, but there was a quiet underlying determination in the way he assured me he was planning on sticking around for a bit yet.

It was obvious to me that we were on the same page, he desired my time as much as I desired his. So many wasted years, so much regret. I tried to explain the look that occurred between us, that one single understanding look but I couldn't find the words to do it justice. No one will ever understand the depth of that exchange, no one except for Daddy and me. My biggest fear now that I'd found him was losing him before I had the chance to get know him. I needed to give him a reason to keep going for as long as possible in order to buy more time with him. My heart ached heavily thinking about it.

'Will you take compassionate leave?' Samantha asks.

'Yes. I would have just stayed this time but it could be weeks or even a couple of months Jack said.' As weak as Daddy looked in himself, I didn't honestly think he would leave me yet. I had two weeks booked off for Christmas, I could finish up early and take three weeks. That would give him something to aim for, something to hang on for. I couldn't bear the thought of him giving up just yet.

I was on the staff rota to work Tuesday, Wednesday, Thursday and Friday that week but I thought to request Thursday and Friday off and head back to Galway for four days.

Samantha understood me more than I could appreciate until now, having lost her Mum at such a young age. She was like a sister to me, her friendship was invaluable. Her sense of empathy so strong, she'd cried with me, laughed with me and despaired of me over the years. I hoped to be her bridesmaid next year and although she was yet to officially ask, it was kind of assumed. If she had her way, she'd be returning the favour shortly afterwards. Often we didn't even have to talk, we operated on the exact same frequency. Friends like that are hard to come by. I knew I was going to need as many as I could get in the not too distant future.

In preparation for dinner with Samantha's friend Daniel, I showered and picked out a slim fitting navy jumper dress, pretty but plain, it was only Sunday night after all. I put thick shiny black tights on and attempt to detangle my unruly mane.Scrutinising my reflection in the full length mirror on my bedroom wall, I examined my features hoping to see some trace of Daddy there, but I simply couldn't. All I could see was the same old me that I'd looked at for the last twenty eight years. It seemed ridiculous but I wanted to see him in me, proof of his life in me, something to hang on to.

Dinner was booked at the hotel Daniel was staying in for seven thirty. Rebecca was meeting us there. Katie was sure she had a fella on the go because we'd barely heard from her for the last two weeks, but she refused to comment on the situation each time we'd asked.

I took the opportunity to make a quick phone call before we left. There was a lot of comfort in being able to phone him, to hear his voice. He answered after three rings.

'Daddy?'

'I'm still here.' He said coughing down the phone. I pulled it away from my ear so he didn't deafen me in the process.

'Are you ok?' I hated the anxious tone emerging from my voice.

'Tired as usual but I'm enjoying that book you left me. Those yokes you stick in your ears are great.'

'I'm so glad you're getting use out of them.' It eased my guilt of being away knowing that he was occupied, not just staring at the four walls.

'Sheila was here.' He informed me. Sheila was his sister, He too comes from a massive family, like Mammy. We had more cousins and second cousins than hot dinners.

'I'm glad you've had visitors.'

'I'm feckin' not! They stand around me mourning me like I'm already feckin' gone!' He rasped making himself laugh out loud in the process.

'Daddy! They're just worried about you!' I hadn't seen Sheila in a few years but I was glad he had at least kept in touch with some of them. They were all a big family of drinkers. Three of Daddy's brothers owned pubs in Galway City and Sheila owned a betting shop.

'They're a feckin' pain in my ass.' He said, though he was secretly delighted that they had all come together for him again. However, if he admitted that out loud they'd know he was really on the way out. They'd have the Priest there within the hour to say the final prayers. I chuckled despite the darkness of our family's situation.

I bid him goodnight and figured if I made a plan for Christmas he would do everything in his power to honour it. An overwhelming sense of privilege at the thought of being given a second chance overcame me making me teary again. It utterly sickened me that there was an unspecified limit on the time we had left together. But then I guess everyone has an expiry date, the only difference is some people are made aware that theirs is looming.

CHAPTER ELEVEN

—

Tuesday 17th November 2015

Occasionally we get asked to cover the Antenatal Clinic, when there is a staff shortage on the clinic below and the next day was one of those days. In the NHS there is pretty much a shortage of everything, although as a service it is still the best in the world. Which was one of the reasons that I didn't want to head back to Kinvarra for what could be weeks or months, it would increase the pressure on everyone. We had a great team, it's not that they wouldn't understand. The thing is, I knew I was going to need that time off later, as the inevitable end approached.

The Antenatal Clinic was easier in some respects, although we saw more patients, there was less urgency. I appreciated the change of scenery, it was a different experience only being able to see the baby on an ultrasound and feel them through the thickness of their mother's womb. It was amazing what you could feel when you knew what you were looking for. As a student midwife it took me ages to figure out the baby's head from its arse, literally. Now it comes as second nature.

I scrolled through the day list on my computer, there were forty eight women booked into the clinic that morning and only myself and Steph there. We'd get through them eventually but it would more than likely mean no lunch again. My appetite wasn't what it used to be anyway.

The waiting room was busy already and I resigned myself to the fact that I needed to crack on with the day.

'Emma McLeod' I shouted as I called my first patient in for her appointment.

A petite, dark haired girl stood up and shuffled in behind me and closed the door tightly. I nodded at the bed and she took her place quickly.

'My name's Orla. I'm one of the midwives here. How is the pregnancy going for you?' Her notes were clearly visible on the screen in front of me detailing her medical history, her booking blood test results and diabetes check. They were all clear.

'Okay I guess. It's the first for me so I've nothing to compare it to.' She shrugged, one hand protectively over her little bump.

'How many weeks are you now?' I asked her.

'Thirty three.'

'Did you bring a urine sample?' I ask.

She produced one from her coat pocket, far easier to come prepared than to have to walk back out through the busy clinic with an empty piss pot whilst everyone awkwardly looked the other way. She handed over the sample and I dipped it with a test stick. We checked the sample at each appointment for glucose, proteins and other signs of infection. This sample was perfect.

'I'll check your blood pressure next, if that's ok?' Consent is everything in this profession.

'Of course.' She slipped off her coat and lifted her oversized sweater in order for me to examine her. I washed my hands vigorously at the sink, positioned the black band around her arm and waited a few seconds for the reading.

'Blood pressure is slightly low but's that's normal at this stage. Keep up the fluid intake, it will prevent you from feeling faint.' I stated.

'Now, I'm going to have a little feel, we'll see which way the baby is lying and listen to the heartbeat.' I show her the Doppler, sending up a silent prayer that everything would be ok.

A few months ago, a Mum arrived on this very clinic, she was at thirty six weeks gestation. I could not for the life of me find a heartbeat. Her toddler ran riot in the examination room whilst her husband struggled to park the car outside, oblivious to the impending tragedy. I nervously paged Dr Sanderson who couldn't find a heartbeat either. The scan revealed the worst, confirming our deepest fear; there was no heartbeat. My own heart broke that day for that woman. Every tragic story I've witnessed I carry forever, weighted on my soul. There are so many more happy endings than sad, but breaking that kind of news is the absolute worst part of this job. No amount of training could prepare you for it.

I positioned my hands around Emma's bump feeling gently for the position of the baby.

'The baby is breech.' I conclude. 'There's still time before the due date though and the baby is moving constantly so it doesn't mean much at this stage.'

'She was breech at the previous two scans as well.' She informed me.

'She? You found out already?'

'Yes. I hate surprises.' She shrugged again.

'Congratulations, it's nice to be prepared.' My standard answer in these situations.

'What if she stays breech?' Emma asked.

'If she stays breech the Consultant will more than likely offer the option of trying to turn the baby, which sometimes works, resulting in the possibility of a natural delivery. Or he may suggest a C-section. Either way it will be discussed with you and planned in advance. Try not to worry about it, she may turn herself before the time arises'

'I'm not worried!' Emma said, stifling a giggle. 'I'd actually prefer a C-section! I quite like my lady bits the way they are!'

After seeing what some women go through, there are days where I feel the same!

'As long as you are both healthy, the rest will work itself out.' I reassure her.

The Doppler picks up a good, strong, healthy heart beat much to Mum's relief and mine. I took out a tape measure and checked the growth of the bump compared to her gestation. It all looked good. I thought that if the rest of the morning were this straightforward I'd be laughing.

Fifteen patients later, with barely any breathing space, let alone time for a pee, I heard a gentle tap on my door.

'Come in.' I say without taking my eyes from the computer screen, scanning the notes of my next lady.

'Hey.' A familiar deep Dublin accent interrupted me. .

I spun rapidly round on my chair and awkwardly patted my messy bun. Tom looked particularly sexy this morning in a tailored black suit and slim fitting white shirt. Palpitations consumed me as flashbacks of Friday night overrode any sense I previously held. The blush crept up my neck line as I pictured my hands desperately pulling him harder towards me. He grinned, flashing his perfectly straight ivory teeth, acutely aware of my less than professional thoughts.

'How was your weekend?' I asked, crossing my arms protectively across my chest as I struggled to compose myself.

'It started off particularly well, one of the best in fact.' He winked at me knowingly. 'But after an initial peak, it was rather dull to be honest. How about you?'

96

'Grand. Well, the same.' No point in weighting him with the truth, it would be awkward and I certainly didn't want his pity. He was intended as my distraction, I wouldn't divulge my situation, it was futile. The time I spent with him was meant to be fun.

'I brought you this.' He handed me a cup of black coffee in a takeaway cup from the canteen.

'Thanks.' I gratefully accepted it, knowing all too well it was the only one I'd get all morning.

'Don't say I never do anything for you.' We were both well aware of exactly what he did for me, the chemistry crackled immeasurably between us. There could be no doubt of what he did for me.

I took a swig of the coffee and tried desperately not to choke on it.

'I'll see you tomorrow?' He confirmed.

'Looking forward to it.' My eyes found his, the explicit promise unmissable. As he left the tiny room without another word, desire spread through my veins like wildfire. Tom Rourke could be a very dangerous man to become infatuated with and least of all because he was leaving in a few short weeks. But that was exactly what was happening.

One patient rolled into the next ensuring another whirlwind of a day. The highlight was undoubtedly my brief visit from Tom. I replayed it over in my mind whenever I got a free second and even sometimes when I didn't. I managed to escape in order to make a quick trip to the ladies as the clinic began to clear, bumping into a friendly face along the way. There was never a dull moment in St. Margaret's Hospital.

'Well Orla, how the hell are you?' Fred was one of my favourite porters, he was mighty craic for an Englishman and that's no mean feat. Dry shites are what they can often be. He was about sixty two years old, but he clucked around the women on the Labour Ward as

97

if he were one of them.

'Good Fred. How's all with you today?'

'Same old, same old.' He shrugged his shoulders before dropping in, 'I hear you have some news though? A secret admirer perhaps?' He tapped the side of his nose knowingly.

'Nothing escapes your attention does it?' I replied with a smile.

'The receptionists downstairs were taking bets on who the sender was. One thought they were from that Senior House Officer Nathan, another suggested they were from one of the patients.' I said nothing as he stared intently at me continuing in his pursuit of information.

'One girl even suggested they were from that chap that's ruffling everyone's feathers with his bloody audit.'

Okay he had me now, I blushed scarlet, which was becoming a dreadful habit, completely giving me away.

'Ah ha!' He exclaimed. He was so smug he actually hugged himself in delight, rocking back and forth with laughter, his hospital trolley abandoned at the side of the corridor and they were invaluable to the poor creatures waiting down in A & E.

'And how long has this been going on?'

'You don't have to say any more.' Mamma J cut in from behind me. 'Take no notice of him.'

'Nothing's going on anyway.' I lied through my teeth, Hospital Policy dictated we didn't get involved with other members of staff, despite the fact that a few marriages had already resulted from the employees fraternising a little too well in this place. Of course by that stage it was too late. It wouldn't be me though. So I wasn't about to disclose my date. I doubted even Fred could drag that one out of me. Waving good bye to Fred, I continued in pursuit of the ladies restroom.

My shift drew to an inevitable end, shutting down the computer, I discarded my scrubs and exited the stuffy hospital building, delighted to be returning to my own apartment. Having agreed to meet Samantha and Rebecca at East Fountain Bridge for a Nandos and a glass of wine, I was conscious of the time. Both of them were off, which I envied, but I needed my rest days to be grouped together in order to make the trip back to Kinvarra. Pauline had kindly done a bit of shuffling with the rota in order to maximise my free time.

At precisely eight o'clock my mobile phone rang shrilly in my hands.

'Where are you? We're starving here.' Rebecca moaned into the receiver.

'On my way, I'll literally be thirty seconds.' I promised, increasing my pace on the nearby pavement. Following my brisk walk, the artificial heating of the restaurant was stifling. Virgin Active mocked me as I walked by it, not yet managing to return after the last promise I made to myself.

'Sorry I'm late girls.' I flopped down and squashed into the leather booth next to Samantha, helping myself to a glass of white wine chilling in the cooler in the centre of the table.

'Busy day?' They knew too well.

'I was on Antenatal.' I took a large gulp of Chardonnay and relaxed into the easy company of my best friends.

'How's your Dad today? Rebecca asked.

'He sounded in good form. I spoke to him before I left the flat.'

'That's great. Is it awkward?' Rebecca asked curiously, in the way that only somebody really close could.

'I thought it would be, but strangely, no. It's like the years apart have melted away insignificantly.' It was difficult to express but we were both aware of the time constraints denying us the liberty to dissect the past even if we wanted to. It was irrelevant at this stage.

Nandos was a relaxing way to finish the day, I enjoyed the carefree conversation of the girls and allowed myself to temporarily forget my problems. There would be no easy conclusions tonight or tomorrow anyway. Samantha gave it to Rebecca hard about her mystery man, which she continued to deny. There was no better therapy than a glass of wine and the easy company of my best friends.

CHAPTER TWELVE

—

Wednesday 18th November 2015

I decided on a slinky black halter neck dress for my date with Tom. It was almost backless, but from the front it was slim fitting and conservative looking. From behind it shrieked 'undress me!' I completed the outfit with patent stilettoes.

Using seven different brushes I did my best to cover my faint Irish freckles and mask the shadows underneath my eyes. Despite my best efforts, the worry of the situation at home was keeping me awake all hours of the night.

A gentle chime from my mobile alerted me to the arrival of a WhatsApp message.

In a taxi. Be ready in 5.

He'd obviously decided not to come up for me tonight, probably for the best if the previous day's chemistry in the Clinic was anything to go by. I squirted myself liberally with perfume, ironically called D & G 'The One'. That was Samantha's dream, not mine, I reminded myself harshly as I pulled on a knee length black belted coat. I locked the door ensuring everything was switched off, practically skipping down the stairs to wait for my beautiful distraction.

The night was crisp, the sky black, barely a star in sight and no trace of the moon. A taxi pulled up within seconds and Tom opened the door for me. He was freshly shaven, the scent of his masculinity radiating from his skin as he kissed me lightly on the cheek. He looked gorgeous in a light blue shirt, just visible under his leather jacket. I reminded myself it was rude to stare.

'You look beautiful.' He stated, admiring my attire, ever the charmer. A small grin crept onto my face making me grateful for the darkness. The blushing was becoming an embarrassing reoccurrence, revealing much more information than I'd prefer.

I glanced at Tom shyly but intently, paying zero attention to the direction in which the taxi was travelling, the air charged with possibilities for the night ahead. He took my hand in his, igniting every nerve ending in me. His touch affected me so powerfully it was practically painful, his strong warm hands full of promising potential for the evening.

We pulled up on a small dimly lit cobbled street, Tom paid the driver and took my hand, helping me out of the car. I prayed I wouldn't snap my stiletto on the uneven cobbles, or worse, my neck. He took my arm firmly, leading me to the entrance of The Tower Restaurant where a young looking, attractive woman appeared to greet us, wearing a crisp white shirt, black satin waistcoat and black tailored trousers.

'Reservation for Rourke.' Tom informs her. That Dublin accent was really growing on me.

'Sir, Madam.' She acknowledged both of us with a polite nod.

From along the corridor I could hear the gentle tinkling of a piano and a soft jazzy female voice singing seductively in the background. As the song ended a light round of applause ensued. With a firm grip on my hand, Tom lead me through the corridor behind the waitress, the dim wall lights creating a romantic ambience, a relaxed warm setting for the night ahead. I prayed they would provide cover for any more of my embarrassing blushes.

She brought us to the huge dining room, where twenty perfectly set tables were generously spaced out to provide a suitable amount of privacy for each couple. The ivory wainscoting matched the tasteful neutral décor from the corridor. Four grand crystal chandeliers hung low from the ceiling. At the front of the room there was a low stage with a piano situated on the left. A blonde haired woman posed behind it wearing a tight black dress with a split revealing the full length of her right leg. She cupped a microphone seductively in one hand, occasionally brushing it with her lips.

I was awe struck, it was absolutely beautiful and truly sophisticated. It was a million miles from where I had been reared in the countryside, this restaurant oozed elegance, reminding me of a scene from a Marilyn Monroe movie. All we were missing was a light smoke lingering in the air, but that had been banned years earlier.

She seated us at a table to the left of the stage, half way back which suited me perfectly. I wanted Tom all to myself, although thankfully it didn't appear that privacy would be an issue wherever we were placed. Each table was decorated beautifully with a starched white tablecloth, a multi wick church candle and a small crystal vase housing three simple red roses. She left us momentarily, so we could examine the menu.

'This place is amazing.' I told him sincerely.

'Worth the wait?' He asked, one eyebrow raised suggestively. The direction of almost every conversation kept coming back to that, it was at the forefront of both of our minds apparently.

'Absolutely.' I was desperate to absorb every tiny detail.

The waitress returned with a bottle of champagne that he must have requested on the way in.I glanced around as she poured our drinks, guests of all ages occupied the neighbouring tables. A couple in their seventies sat closest to us. The woman wore a navy blue evening gown and a delicate set of pearls decorated her neck. Her ash blonde hair was short and simple and she radiated glamour. I betted she was a looker in her day. Her husband gazed across the table at her and looked every bit in love with her as he probably always had been. She gave me a quick smile and it was then that I realised I was likely staring. I wasn't used to seeing elderly couples looking so in love, I couldn't help but wonder if there was hope out there for me after all.

I'd never been anywhere so grand and so romantic in all my life. The short spells of dating I'd experienced over the years had been nothing like this. Tom leaned back, watching me take it all in.

'What do you think?' He took my hand across the table and gazed into my eyes earnestly.

'It's beautiful. I can't believe it.'

'It was recommended to me by a friend, he must have known I wanted to make a good impression.' He sat back and stared at me intently, once again making me feel like I was the only woman in the world. The waitress interrupted briefly to take our order then discreetly left us alone once again to enjoy each other's company. Conversation flowed naturally as we sipped the Champagne, Tom had an easy manner which ensured it was effortless to be around him.

'How long will you be here for?' I found myself asking the obvious question, the one question that I promised myself I wouldn't ask.

'A few weeks yet. I need to be well and truly finished before Christmas though. I've an urgent project in Ireland first thing in the New Year. If I could get a head start on it even before then it would be a bonus. A hospital has applied for funding for an extension and I need to have the audit done and the financial report in place before February.' He tells me. 'What about you?'

'What do you mean?' I replied, confused.

'Will you stay in Edinburgh indefinitely?' He asked and I couldn't help but wonder if it mattered to him either way. Maybe he was concerned I'd fall in love with him and stalk him. Fat chance! Well, I definitely wouldn't stalk him anyway. It wasn't my style.

'Maybe not forever, but I have no intention of moving home anytime soon. I'm not ready to trade the city for the country again yet. Kinvarra is so quiet. I like the lifestyle here to be honest.' Each time I thought about moving home the thought suffocated me. I loved the city, the choices it offered, the anonymity it provided. Samantha often said Edinburgh was a village compared to London, but to me it was everything I needed.

'Aren't you going home tomorrow?' He asked.

'Yes.' It came out sharper than I had intended.

'And didn't you go home last weekend?' He asked curiously.

'Yes.'

'That sounds like a home bird to me.' He teased, without any idea of the situation I had presently found myself in.

Thankfully before he sought further explanation, our fillet steaks arrived accompanied by roasted baby potatoes and asparagus. The waitress recommended an Argentinian red wine to complement them. I rapidly sank another glass of water, unable to deal with a headache in the morning on the flight to Knock Airport again.

The food was delicious but it was the company that really had me salivating. As the waitress cleared our plates away, Tom took my hand across the table and began to draw small circles with his finger on the palm of my hand. Alternating the movements, his fingers stroked the inside of my wrist and gently traced the length of my arm. He couldn't fail to see the effect he had on me, the subtle goose bumps rose immediately on my skin in response to his touch. His eyes never left mine, gazing intently through me. I felt exposed under his stare, aware he could see much more of me than I'd ever revealed to anybody else.

This was unique to anything I had experienced before, I was in seriously close to falling and I was in no position to do such a thing.

The classy older lady wearing the pearls smiled at me as we

stood to leave. She wiggled her eyebrows appreciatively at Tom's rear and I heard the gentle tinkle of her laughter as we passed by her table, Tom lead me by the hand again. I smiled conspiratorially in response and offered her a jovial wink, I couldn't help it. She laughed out loud.

Under the darkness of the cold night sky, the words, 'My place or yours?' escaped my lips involuntarily. Placing his arms under my coat, he wrapped them tightly around my waist and placed his full lips over mine, his desire as palpable as mine.

CHAPTER THIRTEEN

—

Friday 20th November 2015

Glancing around the tiny pub with its tired décor, I noted the same familiar faces that had been sitting at the exact same bar stools for the last ten, perhaps even twenty years. To say McGinty's needed a lick of paint was an understatement. Tourists rarely ventured in, it was actually a hardware shop, come grocery store, come pub, the type that could only exist in the West of Ireland. If you didn't know the bar was here you were unlikely to stumble across it.

Kinvarra Pier boasted several restaurants, a hotel and a couple of bars with enticing views of the water. In complete contrast, this particular watering hole offered darkness and a quiet reprieve from the blow ins, as they were referred to. This was a place to catch up with your neighbours or merely sit in relative peace.

Jack handed me a gin and tonic and nursed a pint of Guinness in his right hand, propping up the narrow wood chipped bar.

'How are ya?' A couple of locals we recognised acknowledged us.Everybody still knew everybody; that much hadn't changed. I used to prefer the tourist pubs before I left, now I enjoyed the quiet solitude of the local that I used to avoid.

'Dad seemed in relatively good form today.' Jack commented, taking a sip of his pint.

'He certainly wasn't any worse than last week.' I agreed, which had been an enormous relief. Although the conclusion was foregone, the previously rapid rate of deterioration had seemingly slowed, for a brief period at least.

'The stubborn git wouldn't go anywhere until he finished those books you gave him now that he's started them.' Jack joked. I hoped he was right, I made a mental note to download some more tomorrow.

Daddy was very sick, there was no denying it, weak and withering slowly, but mentally he was all there. For now that was a positive though I'd come to question that as the end approached. A shudder vigorously swept the length of my spine and I shook it off involuntarily. One day at a time was what we had all agreed.

'So how is lover boy?' Jack teases.

'I don't know what you mean.' I can't quite look him in the eye.

'Mammy said you had some fella on the go, don't hold out on us now! Jesus, Orla he's not one of those fella's in a skirt is he?' He punched me lightly on the arm in the way that only a brother could.

'Careful, you're not too big for a head lock!' I warned him, both of us knowing he most definitely was too big for a headlock and had been since he was about fourteen.Like most siblings we'd a fought as kids, but most of the time we'd been firm friends, valuing the stability of each other's company after Daddy left.

'So?' He continued to probe.

'No.' I said simply.

'No, as in he's not one of those fella's in a skirt or are you still denying his existence?' He was like a dog with a bone.

'He's not one of those fella's in a skirt. They're called kilts anyway.' I reminded him, a slow smile spreading over my face.

'Holy feck Orla. Are you feeling okay? You just talked about a man you are dating with a smile! The Ice Queen herself may actually be thawing.' He teased.

'Just because you'd give it away to any poor unsuspecting girl that looked sideways at you! Some of us have standards!' I pointed my index finger at him accusingly, my tone light, but the truth of my statement was undeniable nevertheless.

Jack liked women. And women liked Jack. He was charming, witty, handsome, but that was where it stopped. He had commitment issues and wouldn't commit to one woman, openly refusing to make promises that he couldn't keep. He clearly warned any woman he dated from the beginning that he was not looking for a long term relationship, claiming the law firm was his one true love, at this point in his life anyway. If you ask me, he just got bored easily.

It was different for me, previously I'd always preferred the company of my friends to most men, no matter how pretty the packaging. I'd never met a man interesting enough to make me want to pursue him, nor had the desire to seriously look for one. I figured I'd made my choice years earlier when I chose my career over the promise of a ring.

'So he's not a man in a kilt... Who is this mystery man?' He mused, intrigued.

'He's actually Irish.' I take a large mouthful of my Hendricks and wonder why on earth I am disclosing my secrets to my big mouthed brother of all people. It felt surprisingly good to talk about Tom, despite the fact it wouldn't be a long term thing.

'This sounds promising.' Jack leans in for more details.

'Don't get too excited. It's not serious.' I informed him.

'Why not? Frightened you'll get hurt?' He teases, never a truer word said in jest.

'He's moving home soon. It's a short contract in Edinburgh.' I tell him simply.

'And where exactly is home?' He asks.

'Dublin.' I reply.

'He's a Dub?' He says outraged. 'Jesus, you'd have been better off with one of those men in skirts after all Sis!' He joked slapping his leg, amused at his own humour. It all boiled back to the football or the hurling in this country.

The pub door opened allowing a draught of cold sea air to blast across the poorly insulated area. Two burly looking men walked in and crossed the small room to the bar to order drinks. Jack raised his eyebrows meaningfully at me and I craned my neck awkwardly to get a better look, locking eyes with my very first love, Daragh Dunleavey. He arrived with his cousin Jimmy in tow. Of all the nights, what were the chances?

'Well! Look at you.' Daragh acknowledged me heartily with a huge toothy grin and an enormous bear hug. There was certainly no awkwardness, from his perspective at least. It was weird coming face to face with a man I once thought that I'd loved.

'Long time no see.' I kissed him on the cheek wondering how this was going to play out. Ten years had flown by and I wondered if he would create the unhealthy stirring of butterflies in my tummy. I hoped not but I couldn't fully trust that it was gone. On the darkest of nights, until very recently, I hated to admit it had been him I'd thought about when sleep eluded me.

This man was my first love, probably my only love. Despite my protests whenever Mammy brought up Daragh's name in conversation, it touched a nerve I didn't like to admit I owned, the thought of him with his girlfriend and their beautiful children evoked a flicker of envy. Not that I wished I was the mother of his children, because I didn't. But at the time when we were together it seemed like a very distinctive, though very distant possibility. He had said it, not so much as an outright proposal but more the suggestion of it, if only I would only come home. I couldn't do it at that time in my life. I had made my decision and it wasn't him.

Selfishly, I had felt hurt when I'd heard his girlfriend was pregnant, despite the fact I wasn't even broody. I'd chosen my career over him, my new life over my old one. I couldn't expect him to simply wait around, yet it had momentarily stung. I'd forced myself to get a grip, cross for behaving irrationally and unjustly. The handful of times I'd bumped into him over the years had been either in passing in the street or when he was with his young family. I'd greeted them all politely and swiftly moved on as quickly as possible.

'How the hell are you girl?' He stood back and took in the length of me from my long red hair to my black five inch heels.

'Grand, thank you. How is that beautiful family of yours?' I asked politely and to remind both of us of their existence.

'They are great thank God. They keep me busy. Our Lilly is getting a handful.' He referred to his eldest and neglected to mention what I already knew, number three was on the way.

'A sign of health.' I nod. It's the longest conversation I've had with him in years and funnily enough, the least awkward.

'You're looking well Orla. It must be that Scottish climate.' He joked but his compliment appeared genuine.

I don't do compliments well. Jack shakes his hand warmly and Daragh offered to buy us a drink.

'No thank you.' I quickly declined.

'Ah Orla, come on.' He insists. 'It's not often I'd get the chance.'

He is right, but it will never just be one drink, because I will of course get him one back, then so will Jack, leaving us in the same company for the duration of the night. I'm sure his girlfriend wouldn't like it, with our history. I didn't want to rock the boat. But then again, in this tiny village I suppose we were bound to cross paths at some point and it's not like I was hitting on him. I was out with my brother for God's sake.

I accepted the fact that we were out for the night. It would be a long day of visiting at the hospital tomorrow so I decided to take the reprieve while I could.

'Go on then. G and T please.' I accepted, while Jack pulled up two more bar stools

Glancing at Daragh intermittently, I couldn't help but notice he was still exceptionally attractive despite the way in which he had aged more obviously than me. That was a product of the outdoor working life and probably years of sleepless nights with crying babies. His dirty blond hair curled at the sides and his five o'clock shadow was more like a ten o'clock shadow, but he still held some of the old appeal. I paused to check myself. The old draw in the pit of my stomach, the one I usually felt when I laid eyes on him was absent tonight. There was definitely some truth to the statement about never forgetting your first love. However tonight thankfully, to me, that was all he was.

Occasionally, I had wondered if things ever could have been different between us, berating myself with questions such as what would have happened if Mary Murphy hadn't landed in Mammy's house that day, leading me in a different direction. Or, what would have happened if in those early weeks in Edinburgh, Daragh had loved the city as much as me, loved it enough to want to move. Would things have been any different?

It was only when Samantha and Simon got engaged or after attending the wedding of a friend or family member, I'd find these thoughts fleetingly enter my head, though luckily enough they usually exited it just as rapidly. It was pointless wondering, he had his girlfriend and children and I had my life as a Midwife, my friends and my freedom. As fabulous as the memories were, tonight any wondering pang I had previously held for him slowly slipped away.

On the other hand, thoughts of Tom interrupted my evening regularly, relentlessly and a little disturbingly. It seemed he had more of an effect on me than I'd initially given him credit for, enough to give me closure on silly childish notions of Daragh Dunleavey once and for all anyway. I couldn't decide if it was a great thing or a dangerous thing, but it allowed me to enjoy the evening for what it was, a bit of craic with a few old friends and neighbours, with no underlying longing or 'what if's?'

From the way I caught Daragh glancing at me occasionally I couldn't be certain he had entirely reached the same closure as I had yet. Different perhaps for him, living in the same house that we had shared so many memories in, so many firsts. I blushed thinking about that summer before I left. It had been unusually hot, in more ways than one. But he'd encountered a whole new set of firsts since I left Kinvarra, first baby, first to settle. I wondered why he hadn't married her, but I reminded myself it was none of my business.

As the night progressed I checked my phone several times to respond to a couple of texts from Tom. He wasn't one to hound me and that was one of the things I liked about him. I told him I was coming home and he accepted it, no more questions asked. A niggling part of my soul acknowledged the fact that maybe I'd like him to ask more, to want to know more. But neither of us were in a position to be starting something serious. My first love who stood a mere two feet away from me was living proof of what I already knew to be true. Long distance relationships don't work.

CHAPTER FOURTEEN

—

Saturday 21ˢᵗ November 2015

'That nurse keeps giving me the eye. I'm telling you.' Daddy insisted croakily, nodding at one of the young blonde girls charged with his care. He looked exhausted, rings circling his sunken eyes, skin gauntly stretched across his brittle bones.

'Hate to piss on your bonfire Daddy, but I think it could be Jack she's after.' I told him, taking his hand in mock concern.

'Sure, why would she take that lanky buck, when she could have the real deal?' He feebly gestured to his frail frame, even making himself splutter out a croaky laugh in the process.

At least he still seemed to have his sense of humour. There had been no immediate decline in the previous few days. A consultant had asked if he would care to be placed somewhere closer to home. Daddy had told him in no uncertain terms that this was his home now, there was nowhere else to go. His own brothers and sisters were unable to take care of him and he had left Mammy a long time ago. He had accepted this was it, I think he even took comfort from it in some ways, knowing that he was in the best possible hands for whatever time he had left. I was certainly happier he was in a place where he wouldn't be left in any pain and where I could ring for daily, honest reports. I hadn't entirely ruled out packing up and coming home but Daddy and Jack both kept insisting it was pointless. Soon I'd have several weeks off to be here twenty four seven if necessary. Ultimately I would need my job after everything, financial stability being the least reason.

CHAPTER FIFTEEN

Tuesday 1st December 2015

'You're going home again?' Tom asked, over his pasta carbonara in Bella Italia on George Street.

'Yeah.' I took a mouthful of my lasagne, at least a mouthful of food prevented further explanation.

'Is everything okay Orla?' He leaned in closer over the plastic tartan tablecloth in concern, eyes furrowed, closely examining for any clue that might indicate the truth.

'I told you, it's just some family stuff going on. I don't want to talk about it.' I insisted firmly. It was none of his business, he was still my beautiful distraction, I thought of nothing other than him when I was in his company. I didn't need or want his pity, he was leaving in a couple of weeks anyway. I figured it was best to just enjoy the time while we could.

Ironic really that I was preparing to lose two men that I had fallen in love with in the last few short weeks. There was no denying it to myself, although I continued profusely to do so to everyone around me; Samantha, Rebecca, Jack and Breda.

Miraculously Daddy was still hanging on in there, especially considering his initial deterioration at the start of the chemotherapy. The nurses regularly flattered me with statements like it's me that he was hanging on for. I wasn't not so sure, but just grateful that he was.

Breda has been awkward about the situation, understandably it was difficult for her too. I don't think she expected that I would actually forge any kind of bond with my father, let alone that he would still be desperately battling on. She seemed to be torn in two contemplating whether she should visit him or not and although she wouldn't admit it out loud, the signs were there.

She sent some books and a v shaped pillow up to the hospital. Her loyalty to Patrick was understandable, she might have imagined that it would be disloyal to him and all he has done for us if she were to run back to Daddy now. I have my own opinion on what she should have done, but it was her business to decide. Daddy would have loved to see her. He saw things a lot clearer in that time and would have loved the chance to apologise, to try put things right.

My mobile phone rang loudly echoing through the restaurant. It was never out of my hand or my pocket these days, I lived in fear of the day I would be told I needed to drop everything and go. Tom tutted but said nothing as I stood up from the table and took the daily progress report from the nurse's station in Galway City Hospital.

I couldn't tell him. I didn't want to tell him. Didn't want to put him in a position where he couldn't just leave me and move on to his next job without being consumed by guilt. I was better dealing with this on my own.

'How is he?' I asked Natasha, the blonde Australian, urgency creeping into my every word, desperate for reassurance.

'He's comfortable.' That was the standard answer these days. He ate less than a rabbit, fading away in front of our eyes. Mentally he still pushed on, refused to give up yet.

'Tell him I'll see him tomorrow.' I told her, disconnecting the call.

CHAPTER SIXTEEN

—

Sunday 6th December

It was a long old day on Labour Ward, we delivered twin girls to a woman who already had two older boys at home. Then I assisted Dr Crawford with a particularly nasty delivery with forceps, the poor woman was absolutely traumatized and who could blame her? Every delivery is so different, it was one of the reasons I loved my job. I didn't enjoy the paperwork that went with it though of course, so much red tape and arse covering these days, it's unreal.

I ran a steaming hot bubble bath, lit a cotton candy Yankee candle and made myself a hot chocolate. My mobile phone was deliberately positioned on the toilet next to me, as ever I was terrified of missing the call that would inevitably be coming. Adele's album 19 drifted through the speakers from the sitting room and I relaxed back into the hot water and took a large mouthful of Cadburys, savouring the taste as it slipped down my throat easily. It reminded me of my childhood, walks in the woods, the snapping of twigs under colourful wellies, followed by a hot chocolate with Breda in front of the open fire.

My mind churned constantly, offering me very little reprieve, I knew change was coming. The control freak that I had become hated that I had no idea of the when and where that would be. Every day I prayed to God to give me a bit more time, even started lighting candles when I passed the Church, something I hadn't done since I moved almost ten years ago, despite my minor white lies to Breda.

Distraction had been following me everywhere I went, nothing seemed relevant anymore. My priorities had shifted. I'd matured a lot and not out of choice. I couldn't stop wondering when the end would come for him, morbid thoughts consuming me day and night despite my best efforts. Working long hours in a hospital didn't help especially as I'd been spending most of my days off in one too. I constantly wondered if he was okay. Wondered how long we had left, wondered if I dared to plan Christmas around him.

It would be magical to have one last Christmas together, even if it were at the hospital. Daddy was too sick to be discharged now, even for a few hours, he neededaround the clock care and anytime the medication wore off he was in agony. It was horrific to witness. It was purely selfish but I had this crazy idea about us bringing Christmas dinner to him, to be a family at for the holiday season, one last time. Would it be too much to ask?It was only a couple of weeks away. I desperately wanted to give us all something to hang on for, romantic and arguably ridiculous thoughts of a family Christmas consumed me.

The only thing, or person I should say, that ever took my mind from my impossible situation was Tom. I was mad about him, or maybe I had just gone mad. Worryingly he was genuine marriage material, not that I'd admit that out loud. He was gorgeous, funny, generous, sensitive and intelligent. We had the same warped sense of humour, possibly from our shared culture or maybe it was more than that. Time spent with him was effortless. From the minute I met him I'd been powerfully attracted to him and from the way he came to me most nights, the feeling was apparently mutual.

There was only one silent, enormous elephant in the room, the teeny tiny issue of him leaving the country. We had avoided the subject like the plague since very early on in our relationship, if you'd even call it a relationship. Both of us well aware of the ticking clock resounding in the background, neither of us willing to address it.

First-hand experience taught me at a young age that long

distance relationships rarely work. My life was here, my job, my friends, my apartment. His life was in Dublin, but he could be sent anywhere in Ireland or Scotland for weeks on end anyway. The fact that he hadn't mentioned his imminent departure spoke volumes to me about our time together, it was what it was.

In some ways I was grateful he hadn't suggested anything other than what it was, feeling the way that I do about the distance, but there was a tiny niggling part of me that dared him to suggest it, to see how things would go. But he didn't and I certainly wouldn't. I regularly reminded myself that it was never intended to be long term, which was foolishly one of the reasons I allowed him to get in so close.

Standing up, I pulled an enormous bath towel around me, tucked it underneath my arms and stepped out of the bath onto the mat on the tiled floor. I selected a cerise pink lace matching knicker and bra set from my extensive and previously unappreciated underwear collection. I pulled on comfy black jogging bottoms and an Abercrombie hoodie. I felt scarily comfortable with Tom, comfortable enough to wear that and comfortable enough to let him sleep in my bed. It wouldn't be easy giving him up when the time came but I wasn't not ready to go the distance, its hard work and I was too selfish. Besides, I repeatedly reminded myself, he never actually asked me to. The buzzer sounded loudly and I pressed the enter button without checking who it was, I already knew.

He knocked lightly on the door, leaning against the outside frame wearing a fitted dark overcoat revealing his expertly tailored black suit. I loved a man in a suit, there was something undeniably sexy about the respect it commanded. His tie was absent this hour of the night, the top two buttons of his slim fitting shirt undone, offering me a glimpse of his lightly tanned body, a body that I was now deliciously acquainted with. He handed me a bottle of Malbec, enjoying educating me in his favourite wines over the previous few weeks. His brother ran a vineyard in France, apparently he'd spent a lot of time there over the years.

'Hi.' I stepped aside allowing him to come in.

'Orla.' He acknowledged me, kissing me fully on the mouth, sending my stomach into overdrive, the gentle thud of my heart quickened, pounding loudly in my own ears as the blood coursed through me.

I grinned from ear to ear at the sight of him. There was something so grounded about this man, he'd long since dropped his mask, revealing his truth to me. He was balanced, steady, and imperfectly perfect. In addition to the fact he had the face of a catalogue model, chiselled and sharp, it was simply effortless to be around him, even if he was a Dub! I groaned internally at the sight of him. I actually thought my Mammy would even approve of him, which would be previously unheard of. Why now? Why him? Why couldn't it just be simple?

His masculine scent enticed me, his tall broad frame brushing past me as he made his way comfortably through to the kitchen and helped himself to a wine glass from the cupboard, pouring us both a generous measure. A part of me loved that he was comfortable here but equally it scared the shite out of me at exactly how easy it was. I'd left a chicken casserole simmering in the slow cooker and it was his turn to sniff appreciatively.

'Something smells really good.' I leaned in to kiss him passionately, his hands travelled down my back and over the curve of my bottom lightly, relaying shivers throughout my core. The abrupt shrilling ring tone of my mobile phone pierced the silence, disturbing our kiss. I pulled away quickly and practically sprinted to the bathroom to locate it. It was Daddy. I took the phone through to the bedroom and closed the door.

'Hello?'

'Hi Pet, it's me.' His voice was strained, talking was becoming an increasing effort.

'Daddy, are you okay?' Aware of the concern in my tone and the pallor of my skin as the blood physically drained from my face in apprehension. I was anxious to establish that he was as well as he had been the previous day. But at least it was him ringing me and not the hospital.

'Same old, you know. Tired, as ever. I'm sick of the sound of myself moaning, tell me about your day. That's what I'm phoning for.' He liked to hear about what I had been up to, about the patients I'd come across or hear tales of my 'wacky friends' as he referred to them. The only news he heard outside of the hospital was the ins and outs of another hospital, ironic really.

I regaled him with the minor details of my day, the deliveries, the craic with the girls. He felt as though he knew them personally at that stage from my regular pictures, boring him with three trillion photos on my phone. Trying to plug the gaps over the years, graduation, my twenty first birthday party, a holiday to New York. I'd have loved to show him around Edinburgh but we both knew that wasn't a possibility so instead I sent him pictures of everything and anything.

'I'll be over Thursday evening.' I informed him earnestly, as ever giving him another date to hang on for. He knew my motives and he indulged me as I dangled the carrot over the proverbial donkey. The truth was it was probably me that was the donkey, but I wasn't ready to let him go any time soon.

'But Orla don't you have a million Christmas parties and things to go to? You don't have to come every week.' He seemed anxious that he could be putting me out.

'Don't be silly. I'd rather be with you anyway. Besides our work party is a Wednesday night, the 23rd of December. But I was thinking I'll come down to you on the 24th? With Jack? We can talk about it at the weekend anyway.' I needn't exhaust him with my plans, planning to broach the subject again on Friday. We both knew that there was a vague possibility he wouldn't make it to the 24th but neither one of us acknowledged it.

'Ok love, you take care. See you Thursday.' He said as he

wheezed painfully, hanging up the receiver.

I returned to the living room where Tom slouched comfortably on the couch with his coat and shoes off. I plonked myself next to him, curling my feet up under my bottom and snuggled in closer. He kissed my forehead lightly and said nothing as we sipped our wine in quiet comfort. Flames flickered atmospherically from the candles, shadows licked the magnolia walls rhythmically and soft music resounded from the docking station throughout the apartment.

After a few minutes he sat up straight and looked at me thoughtfully, unsure whether to voice whatever was playing on his mind.

'Is everything ok?' He asked me uncertainly, taking my hand in his as he had done a hundred times before.

'Everything is fine.' I told him, unsure what exactly he was referring to. It could have been the fact that I darted out of the room every time my phone rang or possibly that he would leaving sometime soon, the exact date unknown to me.

'It's just every time your mobile rings you leap off the chair in terror.' He states matter-of-factly. His cool blue eyes met mine questioningly.

'It's family stuff.' I replied looking at the floor, reluctant to disclose anything further.

'If I didn't know any better I'd say you had a husband stashed somewhere. You never take a call in front of me and you spend half the week in a country that you supposedly left for the bright lights of the city years ago.' He attempted to joke but there was an undercurrent of accusation in his tone.

I couldn't help it, I exploded into uncontrollable belly aching laughter that echoed throughout the apartment, loudly drowning out Adele's crooning.

'You cannot be serious?' I asked, wiping the rolling tears from the side of my cheeks, struggling to compose myself to offer a more appropriate answer. Each time I tried to gather myself to speak the howling took over, spluttering uncontrollably again.

'It wasn't that funny.' He stated, awaiting a real answer apparently.

'Sorry. Sorry… I…' Roaring again I struggled to breathe through the hilarity of his remarks. It took me the guts of ten minutes to compose myself enough to stop laughing as he watched on with one eyebrow raised, contemplating whether I had really and truly lost the plot.

Then I couldn't help it, once I was all laughed out, I cried. I cried and cried, heart breaking, fat, heavy, salty tears, draining any remaining energy I had left. Still I couldn't tell him the truth of the matter. Tom took my hand and waited until I was ready to speak.

'It's Daddy. He's not well.' I refused to go into the details, wiping my nose with a piece of kitchen roll.

'Feck Orla, I'm sorry, why didn't you tell me?' He ran his hand through his dark hair thoughtfully.

'Because it's fine. Everything is going to be fine.' I lied through my gritted teeth. It would be fine one day but that would be a long way away.

'If there's anything I can do...' He trailed off as I raised my hand up to silence him.

'You're my distraction, I don't want to talk about it.' I insisted.

He nodded in silent acceptance, the pieces of the puzzle that was my life slowly beginning to piece together in his mind.

We ate quietly, him a lot more than me. My appetite still hadn't returned with the stress of everything. I was inadvertently waiting for something to happen and nothing good at that. I had that niggling feeling in my gut permanently since I got the news.

I loaded the dishwasher quickly while Tom topped up the wine. I cuddled into his strong firm chest on the sofa, his arm draped gently over my shoulders. My wall had lowered considerably, allowing Tom to see yet another part of me that I desperately tried to hide from the rest of the world.

We watched Jude Law and Cameron Diaz in my favourite Christmas film, The Holiday. I only wished my own holiday would have a fraction of their joy. To me it seemed the future was very bleak.

CHAPTER SEVENTEEN

—

Tuesday 8th December

With so many of my evenings being taken up with Tom, I'd barely had time to catch up with the girls the last few weeks. Tonight Samantha was determined to rectify that, she had invited a few of us round to her place for mulled wine and mince pies after work.

Rebecca boldly stood in Samantha's kitchen, hand on hip, impersonating one of the Dad's from Labour Ward earlier that day who had apparently announced that he'd been delivering calves since he was a boy and he certainly didn't want 'no doctor sticking his hands up his Mrs!'

We roared with laughter, it honestly took absolutely all sorts in that place, he'd been the same man to shake Simon Sanderson's hand after a particularly difficult intervention with the vacuum.

Steph propped up Samantha's kitchen worktop, sipping on her drink, shaking her head in disbelief. The distinctive aroma of cinnamon spices associated with Christmas drifted into my nostrils, in keeping with the season.

'What's the plan for Christmas?' I asked Samantha, who I know was off for a few days this year as well.

'I was hoping to get an invite to Simon's family in Fife for Christmas but he never mentioned it so I decided to make my own plans to go see my father and step mum, even if she is a vile creature!'

Nodding sympathetically, we were fully aware of the tension Samantha faced on her irregular trips to visit her father. She vented as we sipped on our festive drinks.

'I don't know how my Dad could possibly put up with her after having someone as wonderful as my Mum. Janet is so negative all the time, never has a good word to say about anyone. Bitterness oozes from her every word. I think it's because she never had a family of her own, which is hard, I can only imagine, but please don't take it out on the rest of us.'

'How long has it been now?' Rebecca asks.

'They're together three years, I just can't warm to her girls. And you know me, I try, I really do. She doesn't like shopping or eating out, she thinks a woman's place is in the kitchen. She regularly punishes herself with chores, vigorously scrubbing the immaculate kitchen floor, even though she did it the day before.'

'She does sound like hard work.' I say sympathetically.

'She's always making sly digs about how I should be married by now, which is an absolute cheek really considering she was a spinster until she met Dad. I took great pleasure in telling her we've set a date now. At least that should get her off my back for a while.' Samantha said.

'It won't be long coming.' They had picked Saturday the 4th June the following year and Samantha was flat out making plans already.

'I meant to ask you…' She leant in towards me. 'Will you be my bridesmaid?' She asked excitedly.

'Ah! I'd love to! Thank you so much!' I was absolutely over the moon, although I had harboured a secret hope that she would ask. Neither of us having sisters, we had become surrogates to each other over the years.

'Who else would I ask?' She put her arms around me in a warm embrace, her familiar perfume enveloping me.

'Huh Hmmm.' Rebecca cleared her throat loudly, tapping her foot on Samantha's kitchen floor.

'Oh of course I was going to ask you as well!' She said gesturing her over for the group hug.

'And you Steph, of course. You three are my Musketeers!' She raised her glass in a toast.

'Brilliant. Thank you for having us. What an absolute honour.' I really was truly touched, it was the highest of compliments to be asked. It would give me something wonderful to focus on in the New Year, of which she was well aware of, as she linked arms with me companionably.

'So what about a nice peach meringue dress, with puffy sleeves and a few ruffles?' She jibed.

'What about a hen weekend in Amsterdam where you get left tied to a lamppost dressed as a goat?' I retorted, grateful for yet another upcoming distraction.

I wondered briefly if everybody looked for distractions in the manner I do, or if I was just distracting my actual life away. Sometimes I felt I was merely floating, a tumbleweed in the wind, unsure in which direction I was going. It was an odd moment to acknowledge that this might not be normal behaviour.

CHAPTER EIGHTEEN

—

Thursday 10ᵗʰ December

Travelling back to Ireland almost every week had become the new normality for me. I didn't even question it, the flight to Knock was effortless. Tom had offered to pick me up from Edinburgh Airport that evening and I couldn't wait to see him after a depressing couple of days in Oncology. There was no change in Daddy's condition. It was nice to see various Uncles passing in and out and old friends that I hadn't seen in years but it was ultimately a waiting game and we all knew it.

Daddy was worried he was becoming a burden on us, though truly he wasn't. I did my best to reassure him but it was difficult for a strong, once independent man not to even be able to get out of bed to go to the toilet. I felt for him, yet selfishly I still begged him not to leave me.

I had a daft, romantic notion about us spending Christmas together and he knew well that was my ultimate goal. Physically whether he could make it or not was another story, but he was giving it a damn good go. So much so that he'd insisted I stay in Scotland for the Christmas parties and take the first couple of weeks in January off instead. I took it as a good sign, he felt strong enough that he would still be there in January. It didn't occur to me that he was merely being selfless.

As I strolled through the Arrival area, Tom greeted me with open arms. I threw myself at him, pressing my nose into his neck to breathe in his familiar and fabulous scent. He kissed me fully on the lips and took my tiny travel case.

'How is your Dad?' He asked.

'Fine. Thanks for asking.' I felt awkward about not telling him the truth but I didn't want to burden him with the hopelessness of the situation. Sensing my need to change the subject he asked if I was hungry. Surprisingly I was and we decided to go to a Thai restaurant on Frederick Street that we'd talked about trying only the week before.

I enjoyed his company more than anyone else in the world at that time, except Daddy's if I was honest with myself. The thought of losing them both in the near future was breaking my heart but I refused to acknowledge it until I had to.

Tom ordered for both of us, I'd never had Thai before and he seemed to think he knew what I'd like, though I'm not sure what gave him that impression.

He leaned in across the table, the restaurant was relatively quiet but it was midweek in December.

'Orla, can we talk?' He said. My heart felt like it was going to drop into my stomach.

'About the future.' He continued seriously, clearing his throat. He clearly wanted to address the elephant in the room. I however wanted to ignore it for as long as physically possible.

'Do we have to?' I asked childishly.

'Well it might be nice to address it?' He suggested.

'You see Tom that is exactly where you're wrong!' I challenged him defiantly. 'It won't be nice, not at all, for anyone. So really I'd prefer if we didn't talk about it to be honest.'

He sat silently looking across the table at me, surprised at the passion of my outburst.

'We could…' He began but I silenced him unfairly with my right hand

'We don't need to talk about it. We both embarked on this situation fully aware of the score. It is perfectly ok. I won't hold it against you when you leave. I'm a big girl.' I assured him, more confidently than I felt.

'Is that how you really feel?' He asked genuinely.

'Yes.' To be honest I wasn't sure what I felt, only that I wasn't ready to confront it just yet.

'Ok.' He sat back reluctantly, defeated, taking a large mouthful of his Tiger beer.

CHAPTER NINETEEN

—

Thursday 17ᵗʰ December 2015

The girls arrived for dinner and a catch up. I'd made lasagne from Breda's special recipe which included a full glass of red wine and a spoonful of sugar. It sounds gross but tastes divine. Tempting aromas of melting mozzarella, tomatoes and fresh basil wafted from the oven.

'Come on Rebecca! I need cheering up, the least you can do is tell me about your love life!' Samantha whined.

'Why won't you tell us? What's with the secrecy Rebecca?' I added, trying a different tactic. Good cop, bad cop. We'd been at her like this to tell us whatever she was hiding for at least half an hour, well the last five or six weeks on and off actually depending on how preoccupied we were with our own lives.

Rebecca sighed looking resigned to fact that she was about to cave, put her serious face on and we sat up expectantly.

'Okay then...' She leant forward shuffling her bum to the edge of the couch, about to reveal all. I clapped my hands in eager anticipation. Half a minute passed while she inched closer, twiddling with the corner of the cushion. She opened her mouth and both Samantha and I waited with baited breath for the big disclosure.

'Ha! As if! Got thirty seconds of peace though didn't I my little hens?' She laughed devilishly at her own wit.

Samantha was seriously unimpressed and smacked her playfully round the back of the head to let her know it.

'You should have seen your faces! It was a picture. Pure intrigue.' She's nearly crying at her own humour. She really would be crying if she wound Samantha up much more.

'Stop cackling you little witch and tell us what's going on!' Samantha was blatantly miffed.

'When there is something to tell, I will tell you everything, for now there is nothing to tell.' She assured us unconvincingly.

'Of course there's something to tell!' I can't help but raise my voice, frustration apparent in my tone. 'You've got a man on the go, you have done for several weeks at least and you won't even tell us a name! Not even a single detail! Nothing! It's odd. Makes us wonder!'

There was an underlying seriousness in my accusation, a growing tension between us. It wasn't the done thing to keep secrets, we'd become a family over the years, all of us away from home. It may have been unintentional but she was hurting our feelings by excluding us.

'Look it's not that I don't want to talk about things, I just can't girls. Please, don't hound me.' She pleaded.

She raised her hands up in surrender ready to say something truthful. 'I'm worried about jinxing things! You know how I worry about saying too much too soon, I'm trying not to expect too much, not to over analyse things like I normally do and not talking about it helps.' That was probably the truth at least, she was a compulsive worrier. Neither of us said a word in the hope that she would continue.

'I don't want to blow this and I'm really trying here, so please help me! I swear I will tell you everything when the time is right.'

The tension slowly evaporated as her words sunk in, although it was increasingly intriguing. What could be so bad that she couldn't tell us? I worried about her in all honesty.

'It better be worth the wait madam!' Samantha warned her. 'We need the full exclusive ASAP.'

I got up from the couch and put some garlic bread in the oven. My phone rang then,shrilly breaking the moment's silence. I took it to the bedroom to talk to Daddy in peace for five minutes.

After dinner, working side by side the three of us tidied the kitchen, something we had done hundreds of times together in the last ten years. I stacked the dishes in the machine, Samantha wiped the table and Rebecca put the condiments away, singing along to Snow Patrol on my tiny digital radio. We moved through to the living area with our drinks and sprawled out, me on the leather sofa, Samantha on the reclining chair and Rebecca on the floor in front of the fire.

'What are you wearing to the Christmas party? Can you believe it's only a week away?' I asked them.

'No idea.' Rebecca says.

'Tom won't be there.' I tried to drop it in casually, as if it didn't matter, when in reality the thought of it was eating me alive.

'Why not?' Samantha asked.

'His work here is almost finished, he has a trillion other hospitals that he needs to audit as well, it's a massive project. He'll be gone by the end of the week. Headed back to company headquarters in Dublin I guess.'

'Oh my God! I can't believe he will be gone! What are you going to do?' Rebecca exclaimed. I don't know why she was so shocked, we all knew the day was coming. Although I was a little less prepared for it than I thought I would be, the last thing I wanted to do was let them see it. Best friends or not, it felt too personal.

'What do you mean, what am I going to do? Nothing of course!' I told them seriously.

'You mean you're not going to visit him? He's not going to come back for the weekends? You're not going to carrying on seeing each other?' Rebecca seeks further clarification despite the fact that it's exactly what I've been saying all along. In fact I probably wouldn't have got involved in the first place if there wasn't an expiry date on it. I didn't do relationships, not up until then anyway.

'I told you before I won't do another long distance relationship, look at how the last one turned out. Plus I've got so much else to think about right now I can't deal with anything else. It wouldn't be fair on any of us.' I didn't mention the fact that he hadn't exactly asked to carry on seeing me. I couldn't be sure which direction he was going to go in the other night in the Thai restaurant and I couldn't bear to find out either. It was an impossible situation regardless.

I stared into space as Samantha and Rebecca sat silently, temporarily at a loss for words. The two of them thought I was barking mad. Tom was drop dead gorgeous, he was a rare find in an age where all anyone seemed to want was a Tinder hook up. They clearly thought I should be chaining him to the bed or stopping him in any way that I could.

'So what about you?' Deliberately changing the subject, I looked to Samantha sat with one leg crossed over the other, semi reclined, making herself right at home.

'What are you going to wear? I'd say that's the first time your legs have been crossed in weeks by the way!' We laughed out loud the three of us, lightening the mood.

'Got a little black number that I picked up in a vintage boutique in London about three months ago that I haven't even tried on yet, found it in the back of the wardrobe the other day with the tags still on it, I'm so bad for that!'

'Ooh what's it like?'

'It's just divine! I'll show you it at the weekend.'

'Looking forward to it.' I told her supportively.

'I meant to tell you, Simon invited me home with him for Christmas! Well actually he just assumed I was coming, like it was a given. He couldn't believe that I didn't just assume I was going with him now that we're engaged. Plus he knows how I feel about Dad and Janet.'

'Well that is absolutely brilliant.' I told her, hugging her warmly.

'I'm glad I didn't offer to work for Steph this year, it was on the tip of my tongue to offer to cover for her.' Samantha said. She was one of the very few midwives who usually willingly offered to work Christmas Day. Christmas would never be the same for her without her Mother.

'I'm just looking forward to a night in a castle.' Rebecca reminded us of our own upcoming Christmas party for three, something we did annually. It was our time together before we all went our separate ways for Christmas. We'd decided to book a spa day and night at Stobo Castle, set in the Scottish Borders, in the countryside surrounded by rolling hills and mountains. It's so beautiful even the professional photos don't do it justice, everybody should go once. A glass fronted swimming pool overlooks miles of deserted rural countryside, mood showers and individual Jacuzzis surround the main pool. An a la carte restaurant serves every type of champagne and cocktails. I had already checked the website, I just couldn't go if they were one of those healthy places that you couldn't even get a drink! To top it all off there were twelve different types of massages available plus the usual facials, manicures, pedicures and mud wraps which promised inches off your waist.

It was pretty pricey but worth it by all accounts. I had been really looking forward to it, before everything. Now I was worried it was more time away from Daddy, but he insisted that I go, it was only one night after all.

CHAPTER TWENTY

—

Saturday 19ᵗʰ December 2015

It had been the usual week of shift work at the hospital, Wednesday to Saturday on nights. It was no joke but it had to be done. Women had babies every single minute of the day, regardless of morning, noon or night.

Things had been unusually tense between Tom and I after he broached the subject again of his imminent departure. Unsure which direction he was going in when he raised the subject that night, I was frightened to find out. Even if he had wanted to continue, it wouldn't work out, long distance never did. And if he hadn't wanted to, I would have likely taken his head off for rejecting me. So it was probably best left unsaid.

Half of me desperately wanted to give it a go, he was everything I wanted in a man, although I had only just realised it. The other half of me knew better, knew long distance relationships don't work, aware that soon I would be spending an increasing amount of time with my father, watching him deteriorate further. There was simply no time for anyone else at this point in my life. It wouldn't be fair on either of us.

However, that didn't stop my stomach doing somersaults each time I caught a glimpse of him in the hospital corridor or across the canteen. As we'd meet each other's eyes I'd get flashbacks of him lying in my bed or standing naked under my shower. He was incredibly sexy and as the weeks passed he drew me in further to him.

Sadly it was more than likely it our last night together. He had a flight booked to Dublin the next morning, in fact all of the Audit team were leaving so they'd arranged leaving drinks for that night. I should have been there long ago but I found myself dithering around the flat, unsure what to wear to leave a lasting impression for what would probably the last time I would see him.

Taking a good long look at myself in the full length mirror, I admired my long auburn hair set in voluptuous bouncing loose curls extending halfway down my back, carefully styled with the curling tong. Eventually I settled on a black midi dress, classically simple, teamed with shiny black stockings that I knew he would appreciate.

Despite my best efforts and the bravado I displayed to the girls, I couldn't fight that sinking feeling of sorrow creeping in,a pang of the oncomingloneliness that I would no doubt experience when Tom was gone for good. Deflated, I left the house for Tonic, the same bar in which we'd first spoken, armed with my umbrella as my only defence against the pouring rain.

The bar was packed and I scanned it briefly in search of Tom. The audit team were a large one and it would seem in the few weeks that they had been around they had made many friends. I caught sight of him at the bar talking to one of the nurses from the Paediatric Department. She was a pretty young brunette. Tom seemed to be enjoying himself, appearing engrossed in whatever she was saying. A sharp stab of jealousy pierced my chest, taking me back. She seemed keen on him, one hand brazenly resting on his arm as she laughed a little too enthusiastically for my liking at an undoubtedly witty one liner he had just delivered.

Sensing he was being watched he turned to look across the bar at me, the tightness in my chest lifting swiftly as I saw the very deliberate and lingering manner in which his eyes rested on me. Excusing himself from the nurse immediately, he made his way towards me, kissing me on the lips fully while arms enveloped me. It hardly mattered who saw anymore now that the work at the hospital was complete.

I couldn't help but feel selfishly smug as several girls in the room raised their eyebrows at the sight of us together, wide eyed, jaws on the floor. I felt like shouting from the rooftops 'He's mine!' But in actual fact he wasn't mine, maybe he would be if I wanted him to be, but I hadn't the courage to find out. I again reminded myself the timing was all wrong.

'Hi baby.' He murmured in my ear. His breath smelt of Jack Daniels and Coke, it had become a familiar smell which I'd come to love. In fact I loved everything about him. The way he was so in tune with me, he knew instinctively when to kiss me and when to leave me alone. And he was just so damn attractive as well. He looked down at me with those big powder blue eyes, his happiness at seeing me was a double sided coin. We were both fully aware our time was coming to an end. I could see the underlying sadness behind the mask, mirroring my own feelings on the matter. But it didn't change the logistics of the situation.

'You enjoying the party?' I glanced briefly towards the nurse at the bar, but the underlying jibe was noted.

'Her? Are you kidding me? You're not jealous are you? No way! You must care after all!' He said, smiling from ear to ear, over the moon to see that I had a touch of the green eyed monster.

'I was only joking. It's none of my business anyway! And you know I care, don't be like that.'

'Come on beautiful, let's get you a drink and let our hair down a bit. Who knows when I might be able to buy you a glass of champagne again.'

We stood at the bar and Tom ordered a bottle of Moet, it was Saturday night after all. Samantha waved at us from across the room, she and Simon had managed to secure a table further back from all the pushing and jostling for the bar. She looked gorgeous in tight black trousers and a classic black backless 'Samantha top'.

Simon's hand rested lightly on her leg under the table. She motioned for us to come over, rolling her eyes at him behind his back. You'd think they'd been married for years.

Grabbing Tom's free hand I lead him past our various work colleagues staring and nudging each other. It looked like no one had guessed who the flowers were from all those weeks ago after all. Steph was true to her word, as I knew she would be. She sat at the bar wiggling her eyebrows at me, chatting up one of the balding porters.

It felt good holding Tom's hand, being part of a couple for the night, even if it does mean I'll have to answer trillions of questions on Monday without him here to take at least some of the rap for it. But it was definitely worth it. He was like nobody I'd ever known before, or was likely to know again. Never once had he pushed me to tell him anything further about my personal life and the situation at home. He just quietly accepted it, understanding my reluctance to discuss it further, respecting my boundaries.

Tom positioned himself next to Simon, shook his hand and the two of them began discussing the football results. He was scarily comfortable with my friends, nothing phased him. Yet another pro to add to the list of amazing traits that I would miss. I watched as he took his tie off and undid his top button, laughing along with Simon. Every minor move he made screamed seductively at me, I was so physically aware of him, I couldn't help it. It was all I could do not to throw myself at him.

'Hello! Earth to Orla! Come in Orla Broder, come in!' Samantha poked me in the leg with her index finger.

'Ow!' The boys looked over at my yelp.

'Now, now, play nicely girls!' Tom joked.

I turned to Samantha, 'I was listening really.'

'No you weren't you bloody liar! You were watching him taking his tie off and salivating everywhere, now wipe your chin, pick your jaw up from the floor and we'll start again!'

'Sorry. Did you have a good day?' I asked, well and truly busted by my best friend

Samantha asked after Daddy. We discussed what we'd packed for Stobo Castle and the treatments booked. The boys appeared very interested all of a sudden, probably frightened they were missing something, which of course they were. Tom seemed particularly interested in where we were staying tomorrow, although I wasn't not sure why as he would be on the first flight back to Dublin.

Rebecca arrived later than anticipated, shit faced already. She'd been out for lunch with a few school friends that were down from Dundee and had consumed several bottles of wine throughout the afternoon and was now on the vodka. Her false eyelashes were coming unstuck at the edges like a couple of battered birds wings, her mascara smudged carelessly underneath her eyes.

Despite her appearance she was on top form. Well, on a scale of one to ten of being drunk, for her, she was only at about six or seven. But that would quickly deteriorate as it always did. When she was out of earshot, Samantha ordered Simon and Tom not to buy her any more alcohol. We always gave her coke when she got to a five or six on The Rebecca Scale, telling her it was vodka and coke and occasionally she even believed us. Mostly though she threw it back at us and called us a couple of bitches assuring us she wasn't drunk, merely having a good time. She never means it and the next day as the inescapable horrors kick in, she usually thanks us for minding her. I asked Tom to give her the coke tonight, thinking she would be more likely to believe it had got vodka in it if it came from him.

I watched them at the bar from a distance as he handed her the coke in a short glass with ice and initially it looked like it worked.

'She's taking the bait.' Samantha said, relieved.

At that moment Rebecca's face turned to one of disgust as she pointedly handed back the glass to Tom. Outraged she loudly pronounced, 'There's no alcohol in that Tom! What d'ya take me for!'

'Of course there is.' He lied smoothly.

'No there isn't and don't you lie to me! You know, I always liked you Tom!' She spoke to him as if she'd known him for years not weeks.

'I always told Orla, I told her, she'd be mad to let a man like you get away! Now though, after this little stunt' She slurred her words in the effort to get them out in the order that she intended, 'Now, I'm not so sure!' She looked meaningfully towards the barman in an attempt to get served.

Luckily for all of us Tom found her remarks hilarious, swearing to her the drink had alcohol in it, even offering to swap his drink for hers if she wasn't happy. She agreed to the exchange and she was momentarily satisfied. So was I as his was also a coke and it was actually for me to give me a break from the champagne for a minute. Unfortunately it wasn't to be so I guess I had to stick to the bubbly stuff.

All around us various work colleague's began to look worse for wear, shots downed repeatedly, with no regard for the next day. Christmas songs enveloped us and fairy lights twinkled prettily around the bar, a constant reminder of the festive season, the most wonderful time of the year. The place hummed with laughter.

Steph practically sat on the balding porter's knee and when I looked closer it almost looked as though she was licking his ear. There was always carnage on hospital nights out, they were a wild bunch, so it had come to be expected. Across the room the pretty young nurse from the kids department had undone most of the buttons on what started out as a crisp, formal looking white shirt and was lap dancing in front of one of the Greek Paediatric students, with his tie wrapped around her head like a bandana.

Another one of the nurses was throwing up outside the front door of the bar, oblivious to the fact that the entire frontage was made of glass. Everyone could see her friend holding her hair out of her face while she brought her lunch up onto the pavement. Nice. Not that we'd never done it! We'd all had our moments, but having been around for several years it was rare we got into a state anymore. Apart from Rebecca of course who was in that moment using an upside down champagne flute as a microphone to serenade two builder types who took the table nearby to us. They were thoroughly enjoying Rebecca's raunchy rendition of 'Like A Virgin.'

'Can somebody try and coax her over here to sit with us again before she embarrasses herself any further please!' I begged the three of them to distract her. Tomorrow she would have full blown anxiety and manage to convince herself that one of these two charming builders might have filmed her drunken antics. She'd spend the next six months scanning the internet looking for images of herself on all sorts of uninspiring sites, trawling YouTube looking for evidence of something sinister. She was rather dramatic our Rebecca.

Simon approached her smiling, luring her back with an invitation to sing Dolly Parton's 'Working Nine to Five'. Samantha told him that was her favourite, she was literally unable to refuse a chance to show off her vocals (and anything else that may pop out during her performance).

Tom took my hand and pulled me towards him. 'Your friend is an absolute scream! She certainly knows how to enjoy herself!'

'Tell me how funny she is when you have to put her to bed.' I said to him seriously.

'No way! But I'll accompany you to take her home if you like?' He offered.

'Okay let's try and make a move sometime in the next half an hour.' Already I was desperate to get him out of here and get him home with me. From the way he eyed my dress I couldn't doubt that he felt the same.

Simon returned at that minute with Rebecca wailing, '*It's all taking and no giving, working nine 'til five, what a way to make a living.'* Her timing was all over the place but she was absolutely hilarious. You couldn't not enjoy yourself in her company, she was an absolute blast on a night out. The only trouble was, she was liable to go down in spectacular flames at any moment.

The bar began to empty as some of the better practised drinkers moved on to a night club. The remainder enjoyed the continuous Christmas music, it was almost impossible not to get swept along in 'Fairy Tale in New York'. For a few minutes I forgot everything, forgot Tom was leaving and forgot Daddy was dying. I allowed myself to be present in the familiarly fabulous lyrics for a few short moments.

The two builders got up, deciding to head to a night club while they still could. Rebecca waved goodbye to her new friends enthusiastically and one of them winked at her and chirped, 'Let me know if you want me touch you for the very first time!'

She was too drunk at this point to process the remark, in fact she was starting to slump over the table somewhat.

'I'll order us a taxi, the five of us can get in one and we'll make sure Madonna here gets home.' Simon took out his mobile and started dialling a local company we regularly used.

'Home? Already? No way! I'm going to a night club. I'm going dancing!' Rebecca stated defiantly, perking up all of a sudden.

'Yes of course you are honey, we are just nipping to yours first to get your eyelashes stuck back down and touch up your make up.' I lied through my teeth, she always fell for that one. By the time we got her in the door she'd likely be fast asleep anyway.

As we waited for the taxi, we downed the last of the champagne. It had been a great night, better than I'd anticipated. Hospital nights out were always the best. There was so many of us and there was always some source of entertainment. I was a little tipsy myself after all the bubbles. Simon's phone lit up silently on the table indicating our taxi was outside.

I assured the taxi driver that Rebecca wouldn't vomit in the back, crossed my fingers and prayed I was right. She did look a bit green around the gills. If she was sick Samantha would catch it in her hands, she'd done it before. Gross, but that's true friendship for you. Samantha was born for motherhood. I looked down to see a bag with what looked like a shoe box in it.

'Where did that come from?' I asked Tom.

'Those two guys that Rebecca was serenading left it. I thought it was new shoes so I picked it up but look.' He opened the bag to show me an old pair of builder's boots. They must have bought the shoes and changed into them.

'Well what are you doing with them?'

He laughed conspiringly. 'Wait and see.'

I offered to take Rebecca up while the others waited in the taxi but Tom insisted on coming in with me. Rebecca was half asleep but I managed to half walk her, half drag her up the stairs and eventually locate her keys from the depths of her handbag amongst a mountain of make-up and a packet of cigarettes. I'd kill her the next day! She knew I hated her smoking; such a revolting habit.

Rebecca's flat was lovely, modern and new, overlooking The Shore and it came with beautiful furniture included in the rental price.

'This is nice.' Tom commented.

'It's lovely. A bit far out for me though, I prefer our end of town. I mean my end of town.' I smiled at him, shrugging as I corrected myself.

Rebecca crashed out on her laminate flooring in the lounge, on her back, snoring gently.

'Help me move her will you?' We each took an arm and hoisted her up and through to her bedroom where Tom left me to undress her. I removed her jeans and her massive earrings and placed them on her bedside table, leaving her in the top she had been out in and her knickers, under the duvet. When I returned to the lounge Tom was waiting with the shoe box.

'Will you put that in her bin?' I wondered what he'd brought it up for.

'No.' He laughed wickedly. 'I want you to put the boots by her bed so she wakes up and wonders what the hell happened.'

'No way! She'll kill me!'

'Go on, it will be so funny! If you won't do it I will.'

'She will lose her life! I'm telling her it was all your idea!' We laughed together, poor old Rebecca. She'd see the funny side of it too, I knew she would. That is, if she survived the massive heart attack it would likely trigger.

We positioned the boots at the end of her bed and left sniggering quietly, ensuring the door was locked behind us. Laughing hard like a couple of naughty school kids, we got back into the taxi and Tom relayed his practical joke. Simon snorted uncontrollably and Samantha laughed until her sides ached. The taxi arrived at Tollcross first and Tom and I jumped out, bidding Samantha and Simon goodnight. I assured Sam I'd be ready for eleven in the morning for our trip to Stobo Castle, as I checked my phone once again to find there was no news from Galway.

Both of us rushed up the stairs to the apartment in anticipation of the inevitable, the urgency of the night had crept up on us, our mutual desire increasing by the second. We undressed in the hall despite the freezing cold night, it was hotter than an oven between us. Tom pulled my dress over my head swiftly and admired the Agent Provocateur two piece. He paused briefly to whistle lowly in appreciation, taking a mental photograph, which I had no patience for. I frantically pulled his belt off and undid his trousers, unable to get to him fast enough. His lips were all over me, teasing me, tasting me. I unhooked my bra and allowed it to fall purposely to the floor as he watched me silently. I took both of his hands, placed them on my bare skin and he lunged into a hard, passionate kiss, shocking us both with the force of it. We didn't wait to reach the bedroom.

CHAPTER TWENTY ONE

—

Sunday 20ᵗʰ December 2015

At nine thirty the usual shrill intrusive alarm pierced the stillness of the bedroom. Tom needed to be away sharp this morning. He spooned in behind me and pressed snooze for ten minutes, regardless of the fact that neither of us would be able to sleep on. I was wide awake. This was it. He was leaving me.

His hand crept gently towards me, under the weight of the duvet, around my waist, tracing the outline of my body. We made love slowly this time, appreciating each other's flesh for the last time. Silent tears slipped from my glassy eyes and I wiped them away before he could notice. Afterwards we showered together and I washed his hair, massaging his scalp with my fingers. He closed his eyes, basking in the attention. Both of us were quiet. There weren't words. It was a unique situation, neither of us had intended to get quite so involved.

We dried and dressed quietly, stealing glances at each other intermittently, helpless to the different direction our lives were headed in. I threw on some casual jeans and a V-neck fitted jumper ready for my trip to Stobo. Tom pulled on the previous night's suit and he looked as gorgeous as ever, if a little ruffled. I looked into his beautiful blue eyes and at his five o'clock shadow, studying him, memorising it for the future.

'Orla...' He began hesitantly, taking my hand, kissing the back of it tenderly.

'Tom don't.' I silenced him with one finger over his lips. 'If I'm in Dublin anytime I'll look you up. I have your number. I'll see you on Facebook. It's not really goodbye.' I assured him unconvincingly. He looked down at the floor swallowing hard.

'If you need somebody to talk to...' He began, words hanging hopelessly in the still air.

'I know.' I swallowed hard and cleared my throat.

I made us both a black coffee while he leant against the kitchen work top, as he had done so many times since that very first night only a few weeks ago. I was going to miss him astronomically, it hurt like hell to think about and so I resorted to my usual trick, burying my head in the sand, imagining that it was the same as any other time he'd left my apartment. I had the mental cardboard box at the ready, metaphorical masking tape to hand.

'It's been amazing.' He said, closing the gap between us to kiss my forehead tenderly.

'You're right it has.' I squeezed him tightly around his waist before releasing him again, while I still had the strength. I forced myself to picture Daddy lying weak and wasting in the hospital bed, in the effort to remind me why I couldn't cling onto the man in front of me forever. Nothing was forever. And until recently it didn't even occur to me that I might be a forever type of girl.

I held his hand as he walked to the front door. He leaned in again kissing me fully and firmly for the last time. Every nerve ending screamed at me to do something, to stop him, but I didn't. I couldn't, it was never supposed to be this way. I didn't think I'd actually fall in love with him. It wasn't part of my plan, he was supposed to be my distraction. A distraction from another man who would also be leaving me soon. A man who I needed to focus on, for however long we had left.

He walked down the stairs without looking back as I watched him from the door of my apartment, until he was completely out of sight. I sighed loudly trying to expel that feeling of desolation in my gut. I was empty inside. The apartment was eerily quiet. In the privacy of my own home I howled hot salty tears at the unfairness of the situation, so desperately wishing he could have stayed here in Edinburgh with me forever. It was essential that for once I let it all out, let the emotions run freely, before I attempted to bury it in the compartment I had reserved especially for it.

Rebecca arrived sharply, especially considering the state she had been in only a few short hours ago. The morning was fresh and the dash displayed the temperature as two degrees, although the sun was shining. Blue skies hovered above for a pleasant change in the city that usually reminded me of Gotham. If only I hadn't felt so blue myself. The weather thankfully provided a great excuse to wear my enormous D & G sunglasses in a poor attempt to hide my blotchy, tear stained face.

'Why do I have to drive?' Rebecca moaned.

'Because you're the only one with a car that has more than two seats bright spark!' I replied.

'Yes but I'm the only one that drank my weight in alcohol last night! Please will you drive? Your insurance covers you on my car.' She did have a point.

'Okay, I'll swap with you.' Probably safer that way, Rebecca wasn't exactly the most confident driver and that was when she was sober.

We double parked outside Samantha's apartment and rang her to announce our arrival. I hopped into the driver's seat of the Audi A4 and Rebecca threw herself gratefully into the back, relieved at the possibility of recouping some much needed sleep. Samantha approached the car from her flat, looking particularly festive in a cream bobble hat and flashing Christmas tree earrings.

'Morning.' She said, sliding into the front passenger seat, seemingly unsurprised to notice that I was driving, in fact it was probably a relief.

'How are things?' I asked, deliberately avoiding the impending topic of Tom's recent and very raw departure.

'All shagged out, Simon Sanderson may look like the boy next door but trust me he's a savage.' She laughed.

I couldn't help but giggle along with her though it was mildly disturbing to think of him that way. Especially when we were so used to the polished, professional, privately educated toff we worked with on the ward.

'How are you?' Her tone hinted at the exact subject I was determined to avoid.

'I'm ok.' I lied. Having already shed my tears I simply didn't want to discuss it, preferring to suffer in silence. I reminded myself for the hundredth time the list of impracticalities and complications that led me to reach the inevitable conclusion of not even attempting to pursue a proper relationship with Tom in the first place.

My head told me one thing, my heart told me another with every nerve ending in my body pining for that man. The sensible part of me concentrated on the logic. Blinking hard I focused on the road ahead. He had penetrated my life further than I had intended. His frequent visits, the dinner dates and the sleepovers had become routine over the past weeks, ever justified by the fact that it was okay, because there was an expiry date on the situation, whether I liked it or not. Whilst I was engrossed, enjoying the moment and accidentally falling for him, time had passed, routines had unintentionally been established and from that day there would be a massive Tom shaped hole in my life.

'Well, I won't be sad to see the back of Tom fucking Rourke after what you fuckers did to me last night!' Rebecca piped up from the back, apparently still awake. She lightened the mood considerably with her graphic description of her horrific discovery at the foot of the bed that morning.

'The worst fucking bit wasn't even the boots.' She assured us, sitting up straight to relay the story in all its dramatic glory.

'Go on.' Samantha encouraged her delightfully.

'I woke up at four o'clock this morning in my bed with no fucking knickers on, the boots at the bottom of the bed, and a disposable camera on the fucking floor! I nearly died!' She exclaimed.

I hadn't taken her knickers off, that was for sure. She continued with her story, warming up to it properly.

'I didn't know if there was a random builder I'd picked up in the flat with me or what the fuck happened! I crept into the hallway, brandishing my hairbrush as a weapon, not knowing who I was going to find!' Ever the drama queen, her hands flew around the back of the car as she imitated her actions with a pretend hairbrush in mock horror. Our Scottish friend had missed her calling in life, she should have been an actress. She was hilarious. You could not be down in this woman's company for long. Thankfully I had her for the next twenty four hours solidly.

Samantha was doubled up crying, tears streaming down the sides of her perfectly made up face. 'So you were going to brush his hair if you got hold of him?' She squealed.

'What if he was bald?' I couldn't help but chip in, laughter exploding from me as I desperately tried to concentrate on the motorway ahead.

'You two are a couple of funny bitches you know that? It was the only thing to hand.' She wasn't put off from finishing her story, loving her spot; the centre of attention.

'So anyway, the flat was empty. I scanned every room, lurked in each door way until I was certain the coast was clear. By which point I really needed a pee. And lo and behold, I found my knickers on the bathroom floor right next to the toilet so I think we can safely say the only person that may have violated me, was actually me.' She sunk back into the chair as we gasped for breath, envisioning our paranoid, anxious, safety conscious friend in the horrors at four o'clock this morning.

'Fuckers.' She muttered but she laughed anyway, seeing the funny side of it.

'What about the disposable camera?' I remembered.

'Must have knocked it off the top shelf on to the floor while I was getting ready. Think it was from a wedding last year.' She shrugged. The car fell silent for a while, minus the odd eruption of laughter from Samantha who couldn't remove the image of Rebecca brandishing a hairbrush from her mind.

'How's your Dad today?' Rebecca asked thoughtfully.

'Hanging on. Stable today, but that could change in a split second, you know how it is.' I replied.

As awful as it was I wasn't sure what was upsetting me more, thoughts of Daddy dying or Tom leaving. All the men in my life would soon be gone, what a morbid thought. I tried to focus on Daddy, it kept my mind from Tom at least.

'He's losing weight rapidly as they do. His mouth is in agony, he lives on jelly, nothing else. It's no quality of life, yet I beg him not to leave me yet. Selfish I know.' I admit the truth of it to my best friends.

'And what about pain relief?'

'They just keep upping the doses of the morphine. He's not in pain. At least he says he not.' I added doubtfully as an afterthought.

With our shared background in medicine it was a situation we all knew too well.

'I feel guilty, pleading him to hang on, to stay with me. I think he is ready to go.' A stray unruly tear slips out of the corner of my right eye and I wiped it away with the back of my hand before anyone noticed, hating that I'd turned into a crier.

'He might be ready, but I'm not.' Selfish of me, purely and utterly self-centred. It was an awful situation, the outcome certain at this stage, but I thought 'not yet, please God, not yet.'

The car was quiet as the girls admired the rolling hills and tiny streams in the Scottish scenery, lost in their own thoughts. Rebecca slumped in the back seat snoring lightly with her mouth open, catching flies.The journey passed uneventfully. I felt guilty for not being with Daddy in Galway. He constantly reminded me that I couldn't be there twenty four seven but it didn't stop the guilt that I attempt to brush off unsuccessfully.

The subtle sign post directed us up the long drive to Stobo Castle, a slow climbing lane up to the front entrance, while the three of us stared in awe at the masses of rugged earthy green land where wild deer and rabbits roamed wild. The soothing trickle of water from a nearby stream could easily be heard over the quiet purr of the engine. Other than that, it was deliciously silent. Beautiful. The Castle itself loomed magnificently before us, prominent and proud at the top of the hill, the winter sun illuminating its majestic architectural beauty.

'Wow, this place is amazing.' Rebecca was wide awake now.

I parked the car outside the front entrance and the three of us lifted our bags from the boot, practically racing up the icy concrete steps two at a time into the elegantly dressed reception room.

A fifteen foot Christmas tree towered above us, decorated solely in red and gold bows and baubles with twinkling white, tasteful Christmas lights positioned in perfectly straight lines. An enormous single chandelier hung from the centre of the ceiling, minute crystals reflected thousands of spots light from the sun. Mahogany bay windows boasted cushioned benched seating areas overlooking the magnificent landscape.

The receptionist greeted us pleasantly, taking the car registration and a credit card and pointed us in the direction of our rooms. We followed the wide, winding staircase, admiring the portraits hanging on the walls and the exotic array of vases and flowers, all in keeping with the festive period. Holly wreaths hung on each bedroom door we passed and a light scent of pine needles wafted through the corridor. Poinsettia plants were neatly placed in each window of the long corridor.

'This is it.' I pushed the bedroom door open and gestured to girls to do the same, we had managed to book the three rooms in a row, only because we'd made the reservation last January. The room was about forty feet wide with two king size beds separated only by a bedside table and a gold antique lamp with a wide brimmed cream and wine coloured shade. The walls were magnolia, apart from the back one that the head boards rested on. This wall was decorated expensively with a deep burgundy wallpaper. The wooden furniture was again a lovely dark mahogany. I loved the tranquility the place offered after the city.

I rushed through to the bathroom to search for any other luxuries I could find. A five foot Jacuzzi bath took up a large amount of space and a separate shower in the corner that could easily hold four people (if that's what you were into). Thinking of the one person I'd loved to have shared it with, the sadness crept in again. I mentally slapped myself.

Black and white gleaming tiles lined the walls and pride of place was an enormous mirror stretching from floor to ceiling. Tiny bottles of luxurious Elmis shampoos, conditioners, cleansers, toners and moisturisers covered the chrome corner shelf and I couldn't help but open one and sniff. Momentarily I was distracted from my impending worries.

Samantha knocked, took one look at me and laughed, 'Come on let's go to the spa area, I booked us some treatments.'

'Should I really be here though?' The stark contrast of an image of my father in the Galway City Hospital flashed through my mind, making all this luxury seem inappropriate and undeserved.

'Orla! He made you promise to come! It's been booked for eleven months! He promised you he would be ok.'

'I know. I just feel bad.' I couldn't help it, my thoughts were only natural.

'You've travelled to Ireland every week since you heard. You will be there again in a matter of hours. Allow yourself this tiny reprieve while you can get it. I hate to tell you what you already know, you've had a rough couple of months. Things are going to get worse before they get better.' Samantha said quietly but firmly.

'Jesus, Mary and Joseph. Depress me altogether why don't you.' I attempted to joke but she had succeeded in striking a chord within me. We had access to this luxury for less than twenty four hours. I'd left an empty apartment in Edinburgh and it wasn't like I had a boyfriend to rush back to. I would be back in Galway soon enough for three full weeks at least. I offered up one more silent prayer again that he would hold on for Christmas. I thought of just one Christmas, as childish and selfish as it sounded.

'Are you okay?' She asked, knowing full well that Tom's departure had me in bits though I was too proud to admit it.

'Yes. No. I'm ok. Trying not to think about it.' I told her honestly. Talking about things would mean I'd have to deal with them, making it all too real.

'You have a lot on your plate.' She said. 'Try and give yourself one day off from it all.'

Samantha fluffed up her hair, scrunching it through her fingers and wrinkled her nose, a clear indication the conversation was over.

We changed into our swimsuits, pulled on the oversized fluffy white dressing gowns provided and standard matching slippers and then knocked for Rebecca. On route to the Spa I vowed adamantly to try my utmost to leave my worries behind for one day. After all, there was nothing I could do about things regardless, time is promised to no one. I left my phone in the bedroom for the afternoon, it was the first time it hadn't been within a foot of my body since I received the news. Oddly I felt weightless without it, allowing myself permission to have a couple of hours off. I deliberately turned my attention to the stunning view from the glass wall next to the infinity pool, overlooking the rugged rural landscape, determined to forget everything for a few short hours.

The three of us were unusually quiet, each lost in our own thoughts. Thankfully we weren't the type of girls that needed to constantly fill the voids with words, the silence was actually very comfortable. This would be a lovely venue for Samantha's hen party and I made a mental note to chat to the receptionist before we left tomorrow.

I swam thirty lengths of the pool, absorbing the magnificent scenery whilst the daylight permitted it. After half an hour in the Jacuzzi, Rebecca disturbed my peace, wildly pointing at possibly the only man in the entire complex. She was worse than a bitch in heat. Samantha went for an Indian head massage, returning with a glass of champagne in her hand, declaring, 'What? It is after twelve isn't it? Don't look at me like that!'

I had no argument and simply wondered where I could get my hands on one. She pointed me in the direction of the bar and I requested a glass to enjoy with my manicure. It was so far removed from my recent reality.

I deliberately avoided addressing the hole in my heart, a gaping open wound that I knew I would feel the full weight of once I returned to the solitude of my own empty apartment. Plenty of time for mourning then, all thoughts of Tom enclosed in a cardboard box, separate to the one in which I stored the worries for my Daddy. Mentally I had a foot on the lid of each box, balancing between reality and the truths that I hid from.

The spa suite was divided up into fourteen rooms for privacy, each kitted out majestically with red and gold drapes on the windows, towels and complimentary robes left to hand. The subtle scents of various sweet and musky massage oils lingered in the air and aromatherapy oil burners illuminated the corners of the room. Subtle work lamps cast enough light to display an array of brightly coloured nail varnishes from girly, glossy pink to a deep black cherry.

The beauty therapist introduced herself and ushered me over to sit at the table and consider colours as she began filing and buffing my nails. I decided to go for a bright crimson, it was Christmas after all. Only three more working days were left then I had three weeks off, plus I knew Pauline would give me more time if I needed it.I was tired, the travelling was catching up with me, that and the weight of my worries.

The therapist initiated small talk, she asked where I'd come from and I kept my responses vague, this time was purely for me. She took the hint quickly and worked away quietly at my hands.

In the solitude of the spa my thoughts were unbearably loud, refusing to remain in their respective boxes. Overpowering but intangible, confusing even to me. I pictured Daddy in his hospital bed and desperately tried not to fear something awful happening to him while I wasn't there. The guilt of being away niggled slightly but I was equally relieved with the break, exhausted from the trauma of the past couple of weeks. I didn't begrudge it in the slightest, actually grateful to be given the opportunity, however long we had, but the constant hanging on tenterhooks was wearing me down.

I so badly wanted to ensure we'd have a memorable Christmas together, to make it as enjoyable for him as possible, although he didn't appear to care, it was just another day to him. In fact if I was really honest it was probably more for mine and Jack's sakes, to give us something to hold onto afterwards. Not for the first time that weekend it occurred to me how selfish I was being. Had I always been like this? If Daddy was ready to go, was it fair to beg him to try and hang on for my sake?

It would be odd not having Christmas day with Breda. She said she understood, urged me even to spend it with Daddy. It didn't relieve my guilt. I couldn't win. The trials and tribulations of the broken family. This was the first time I'd actually had to choose, Daddy had never been an option before and the likelihood was that he would never be an option again. So in actual fact, it hadn't left me with a choice at all.

For a fleeting second I allowed myself to acknowledge that Tom would be in Ireland for Christmas. The thought of contacting him was briefly tempting, only having said goodbye a few short hours ago, his touch was soldered freshly onto my skin. I dismissed the idea as quickly as it arrived, promising myself I'd let him be. It wasn't fair, not on either of us. It would be just as hard to say goodbye again after the festive period, the end result being the same. We lived in different countries. But in the dim light of the spa, safe in my secret fantasy world, I allowed my imagination take over for a few seconds and play out a pleasant scenario, envisioning bumping into him in a bar in Dublin as he had suggested we might. I pictured the surprise on his face when he saw me, could imagine all too well how he would greet me and whisper in my ear seductively.

'Did you decide what colour you wanted?' A high pitched voice asked, startling me.

'Hmm?' An image of Tom in his slim fitting suit with the top button of his shirt undone was still at the forefront of my mind, I felt mild irritation at the interruption.

'The colour? For the varnish?' She said to me again like I was thick in the head.

'Oh right yes, I'll go with the red one thanks.'

Back to earth with a bump, I took a sip of my champagne and considered the reality of the situation. Never before had I stopped to consider what I actually wanted out of my life. Sure, why would I? I had been so busy enjoying the here and now, it had never occurred to me. Confronting issues such as my father reappearing out of nowhere, terminally ill and then meeting Tom and letting him go again somehow forced me to contemplate what was important in life. What was the point in it all? What did I want when all was said and done? What did anybody want? Do they even know? I was never the girl parading around with a pillowcase on my head pretending to be a bride, but did that mean that I never wanted to be a bride? I'd never really thought about it before, never had a reason to.

It was deep stuff and it scared the shite out of me. Normally I do what I want, when I want, work hard at a job that I'm passionate about. There could be no occupation as rewarding as mine, I was one hundred per cent sure of it. I had a fantastic social life, a brilliant family. There certainly had been no void in my life in the shape of a potential partner, I was too busy to even consider it. Until now.

There had been a few guys over the years, nothing serious. A few dates, here and there. I couldn't be bothered to chase anyone. Samantha always said I was like an ice queen, advising me to show a bit of interest if I wanted anything to come of it. That wasn't the done thing where I was from; the way you showed somebody you liked them was by calling them a bollocks and giving them a playful punch on the arm. Besides, I'd never met anyone that had inspired me to want something to 'come of it' before.

Try as I might, I couldn't see the big picture, the future. I suppose I never envisioned myself with children, but I equally I didn't envision myself without them either. I stared thoughtfully around the room, seeing everything and nothing, an odd moment for clarity. For now, the priority was to deal with the pressing issues in the here and now and accept the inevitable. I sipped on my champagne and reminded myself not to overthink anymore this weekend. I would not arrive at all the answers in one day but I was grateful for the rare opportunity to reflect. One day at a time. Though I was already regretting letting Tom go, right then I couldn't consider any other option. Outside of my family situation, I had nothing more to give at this point.

Dinner was booked for eight pm. The enormous dining room could comfortably seat a hundred and fifty people, the décor dark, carrying the same gold, green and red festive theme. The three of us gathered at a large table, bronze candle holders supported long thin crimson candles as a centre piece. A thirty foot high ceiling offered a luxurious sense of space above us and light classical versions of Christmas songs emitted from subtly placed speakers close to the floor. The underlying excitement associated with the time of year was easily detected in the air around us, a soft hum of conversation and laughter echoed around the magnificent traditional room.

'Merry Christmas!' Rebecca toasted, raising her third glass of champagne. We gently clinked flutes, the crystal tinkling lightly together along with our laughter.

'Are you okay?' Samantha asked me earnestly. 'Missing lover boy already?' The champagne had loosened our tongues already.

'Of course I'll miss him. But I'm ok.' I would be anyway. Having returned to the room to discover no missed calls or messages, I checked in with the nurses and they assured me Daddy was settled, fast asleep and Jack was on his way. I allowed myself the rest of the night off from worrying, more than ready for a bit of light hearted banter with my besties as it wasn't often we all got the chance.

Samantha was repeatedly topping up Rebecca's glass from the bottle sitting chilling in the cooler next to the table, plying her with the most alcohol, not that she needed any encouragement at all. Tonight was the night we were hoping she would reveal her big secret, the mystery man whose identity she was so protective of.

'Okay Rebecca, let's play twenty questions.' Samantha suggested over desert once she was suitably confident that Becca was at least a four on The Rebecca Scale.

'Okay who will go first?' Rebecca clearly didn't understand the version that Samantha wanted to play.

'You will.' Samantha said, stifling a laugh.

'Wait a minute we haven't even gone over the rules!' I reminded them.

'But we all know the rules!' Rebecca exclaimed.

'No we don't! This is the Christmas version of twenty questions!' Samantha told her.

Rebecca looked confused, the stirring of her suspicion in her narrowing eyes as she glanced back and forth between the two of us. I exploded with laughter, it was a liberating method of releasing pent up emotion.

'Oh I see! You two bitches are ganging up on me again is it that it? Well Miss Broder you better sleep with one eye open tonight, you are already sailing close to the wind following your performance last night!' Rebecca threatened half joking, but if there was an underlying threat in it who could blame her.

Samantha pulled it together looking almost serious again, 'Seriously let's play the game, you only have to answer yes or no and we want to hear about your man, so picture him in your head and we'll ask you about him.'

'I told you before I can't tell you.' Rebecca appeared genuinely distressed.

'You don't have to give us his name, I'm sure we wouldn't know him from Adam anyway. Or do we?' I said, as it dawned on me with striking clarity that I may just have just hit the nail on the head.

'Come on you know you want to tell us about him, just a bit.' Samantha pleaded shamelessly.

'Ok but I'm not answering twenty questions!' Reluctantly she temporarily swayed.

'Does he have a big one?' Samantha started the ball rolling lowering the tone as usual, asking something which wouldn't give anything away about his actual identity, which was precisely what Becca was so obviously protective of. I had no doubt the questions were about to work up to something more demanding in the not too distant future.

'Ha! Easy! It's massive!' Becca laughed holding out her cutlery in each hand in an exaggerated motion, taking Samantha's bait.

'A simple yes or no will suffice!' I reminded her with a laugh. The waiter appeared to offer coffee to which we unanimously and immediately declined. Things were just beginning to get interesting.

'My turn!' I returned to the game whilst we were enjoying relative success. 'Is he younger than you?' Rebecca had a penchant for younger men, in addition to emotionally unavailable ones.

'No.' She replied, as we attempted to mask our surprise.

Samantha fired out another question nudging me under the table.

'Does he work with his hands?'

Rebecca considered this one in her tipsy state unsure how to answer it before finally answering with, 'Yes. I suppose he does.'

She also had a penchant for manual labourers, the dirtier and more masculine the better, so no surprise there.

'My turn again!' I said as the waiter returned with another bottle of bubbles. We paused to listen to the origin of the drink, how and where it was made, without much interest at all, desperate to get back to the game. Rebecca was providing us with much more interesting information. Detecting our lack of enthusiasm for detail, the waiter swiftly departed.

'Did you meet him in Edinburgh?' I asked.

I could see her debating whether she would give too much away but she decided to answer anyway.

'Yes.' She replied quietly.

'Does he have dark hair?' Samantha asked.

'No.' She replied.

'Is he married?' I blatantly asked the outrageous question we'd been desperately concerned about.

'No!' She answered hotly. 'What do you take me for?'

Samantha and I looked at each other both thinking the same

thing. If he's not married what is the desperate need for secrecy? What could possibly be worse than that? We must know him, it was the only other thing it could be. Rebecca reverted to her serious self all of a sudden and the atmosphere changed, almost tense.

A light switch flicked on in Samantha's head. 'Do we know him?' She practically shouted as she reached the same conclusion as I had.

'I'm not saying another word.' Rebecca stated defiantly. 'You already got more out of me than I intended to say! That's it. Leave it there now!' Sobering up at a rapid rate, we'd crossed a fine line.

'I'm going to the toilet.' She said, pushing back her heavy chair loudly. 'When I come back, I don't want another word mentioned about it.' She adamantly stomped off in search of the ladies.

'We must know him!' Samantha exclaimed. 'Why else would it be such a big secret! Do you think it's someone from work?'

'One things for sure, we aren't going to find out tonight. Leave her be. She'll tell us when she's good and ready I suppose.' I refused to rock the boat further on this rare reprieve from the real world.

'On the plus side, at least he's not married.' That had been Samantha's biggest worry.

'Change the subject before she feels we tricked all that out of her, which we did I suppose.' I felt a bit guilty, she was entitled to a life without us, but because we had been so close, living in each other's pockets for the last ten years we felt oddly excluded.

Rebecca returned and we made our way to the cocktail bar adjacent to the reception room and found a Polish barman to have a bit of banter with. Two cocktails later, we were laughing wildly at Rebecca's impersonation of the Polish accent while the barman attempted to teach her to curse profusely in his native tongue, something I had no doubt he would be instantly dismissed for in an establishment such as this. My belly ached from the laughter, the earlier game and my worries temporarily forgotten.

I slept better than I had anticipated, falling into a dreamless slumber in the huge bed, whether I could attribute that to the alcohol or the afternoon in the spa was up for debate. Either way I felt more physically refreshed than I had in weeks and decided a swim would be the best way to work on my mental anguish, which was returning by the second. The pool was quiet this time of the morning, the sun was only just rising over the rolling landscape. Damp drizzling rain trickled down the gigantic windows but the season was irrelevant in here.

A leisurely breakfast was served in the magnificent dining room, every imaginable choice beautifully displayed; pancakes, eggs benedict, smoked salmon, bacon, sausages, croissants, yoghurt and a variety of deliciously fresh fruit. We gathered our belongings and prepared to return to the city, a little more ready to take on the world than the day before. The receptionist took a photo of us in front of the huge Christmas tree as we posed together, smiling widely for the camera. I wondered briefly if I were to put it on Facebook, would it inspire Tom to leave a comment.

During the drive back to Edinburgh the girls discussed plans for the coming week, Christmas was only a few short days away. I was so close to achieving my goal in Galway. The Hospital Annual Christmas Ball was to be hosted by the Assembly Rooms on Wednesday night. Hospital functions were always good fun, the staff knew how to have a good time and there was always some sort of scandal.

Unsurprisingly when I arrived back at the apartment the cold harsh reality of the situation struck me again; he was gone. Tom's aftershave lingered in the air, winding me like a jab in the gut. I stripped the bed sheets and placed all the towels in the washing machine, blitzing the place with the Flash Bleach spray, eradicating any remaining trace of him from my life. Short term, it provided me a sense of purpose, a feeling of control. I wiped away anything that could remind me of a man who was no longer here, a man I could no longer have.

To fill the silence I rang Daddy for the third time that day.

'Don't worry I'm still above ground.' He answered the phone next to his bed on the fourth ring. He wheezed heavily, every word an obvious struggle.

'Keep it that way Daddy. Please. I'll be home for Christmas soon.'

'Is it Christmas? I hadn't realised.' He attempted to joke, coughing and spluttering down the phone.

'Shall I come now?' Concern tainted my tone.

'Don't be daft. I'm going nowhere. You'll be back again soon enough.'

'I will Daddy. I promise.'

'Stop worrying. You'll get wrinkles.' He croaked before bidding me goodbye.

I rang Breda and then Jack, lonesome, attempting to pass the time, desperate to fill the void appearing in my life, in the space that Tom had so effortlessly filled the last few weeks. The apartment was immaculate and it was only three thirty. I decided to take a walk into Princes Street and look around the Christmas Markets. The walls were closing in on me, a sense of panic rising within. With Tom gone and the future of Daddy's certain fate ticking closer, I felt there was an ominous time bomb ready to explode at any minute.

CHAPTER TWENTY TWO

—

Wednesday 23rd December 2015

I had been charged with the care of a women who delivered twins naturally and she had been needing a lot of help to get them properly latched on to feed. There was a mountain of paperwork to face and I'd had a student midwife tailing me for the entire day, asking me three thousand questions of which I did my best to answer. There was no time for coffee and no one to bring me one since Tom's departure.

I pulled my fringe back with a Kirby grip from my starched scrub pocket and typed my outstanding notes up, my fingers banging the keys furiously trying to accurately record the events of the day. It had been my last working day before Christmas and stressed though I was, I was looking forward to getting out of here.

Throwing my blood spattered scrubs into the clinical washing room I felt the relief of a person who knows they are going on annual leave. I worked Christmas the year before and I wasn't doing it again this year, I had too much else to do. I left to get ready for the night's ball.

When I arrived at The Assembly Rooms later that evening it was already packed with NHS staff from all over Scotland. A few faces I recognised, many I didn't. Men sported a variety of kilts and tuxedos, the women wore an exotic array of elaborately styled dresses, all shapes and colours. There was little danger of anyone wearing the same dress as me, a floor length black maxi, because technically it was a bridesmaid dress, worn only once by my cousin Aoife, before she passed it on to me.

I found myself wondering what on earth I was actually even doing there, the only reason I could think of was that I'd promised the girls I would be. Other than that I had zero interest. I should have been at home in Kinvarra by then. It wasn't even like Tom was there to keep me occupied. Glancing around the sea of faces surrounding me, I felt the loneliest I'd been in a long time, despite the crowded room. I looked around for my friends who had already flocked to the bar.

The ball was spread over three floors, the lowest floor being a quieter bar area where you could actually hear yourself think, the first floor hosting a Ceilidh in traditional Scottish form and the second floor offering a disco and three bars. A glittering disco ball hung from the centre of the ceiling, the entire establishment was covered in thick silver tinsel and snow frosted artificial Christmas trees. White fairy lights hung daintily from the ceilings, it was seasonally beautiful.

In true form there were a couple of drunks already despite the early hour of the evening and we watched as one guy pulled his mate outside before he threw up everywhere or somebody hit him for being a pain in the arse.

Simon looked fabulous in his tux and I had a pang of longing for Tom, remembering the sharp contours of how he filled a suit so fantastically, but I had to let that one go. He hadn't contacted me since he left last weekend, nor had I made any effort to contact him. It was probably better that way, but it didn't stop me sneaking a look at his Facebook page every now and then. As far as I could tell there had been zero activity.

Samantha and Simon looked great together, they were very well matched, a handsome couple. They would make beautiful babies one day sooner rather than later if Samantha got her way. Luckily Rebecca was there to keep me company, looking super stunning in a green strapless number. With her by my side I didn't feel like a complete spare wheel. We gathered at the bar with some of our colleagues and Simon's friend Ben, who worked in Glasgow joined us.

Ben was quite cute and I was surprised Rebecca wasn't paying more attention, she must be smitten with Mr. X! The plot thickened. Conversation was light and easy to slip in and out of which worked for me as my mind frequently wandered. It was becoming increasingly hard to focus at that moment with the future unbearably bleak in front of me. Whichever way I looked at it I knew I would be burying my father, sooner rather than later. Not a particularly festive thought. I tried not to think of the inevitable.

The music vibrated through the speakers loudly which at least helped to diminish the small talk.

'So you guys studied together?' Ben asked me sliding in closer, shouting to be heard over the music.

'We certainly did.' I replied, without expressing any real interest.

'Did you and Simon study together?' I asked out of mere politeness.

'We did a lot together.' He laughed, 'but studying wasn't one of them! More like drinking and golfing and that sort of thing, but yes, we were in the same class.'

'Ah. I see.' I nodded, hoping he wasn't coming on to me, couldn't deal with that right then. All I actually wanted was Tom, strong and steady, minus all of the complications. I caught sight of Margaret and George, two of our old professors from our student days. It was rare I got to meet up with them so I was only too delighted to go and greet them. At least I was safe in their company.

'Young lady!' George exclaimed with his usual greeting. 'You look simply fabulous, doesn't she Margaret?' He pulled at Margaret's elbow like a small child until he had her attention. I saw her roll her eyes to the heavens, it looked like George had started early on the wine. They had been married for years, him an Obstetrician, her a lecturer in the University.

'Well there's nothing wrong with his eyes anyway.' She offered loyally as she touched the side of my dress. 'You do look lovely.'

'Thank you Margaret, so do you and George, you make a very handsome couple.' George looked a little awkward in his bow tie if I was totally honest and he was already tugging at it. I thought it more than likely it would be off in the following half an hour or so.

I chatted to several colleagues throughout the evening, danced with Rebecca and Samantha, even once with Simon. I refused Ben's offer, insisting I needed another drink instead, which wasn't strictly a lie. He was lovely, but he was no Tom.

The sharp pang of longing consumed me once again. I had a horrible feeling that letting him go was a monumental mistake. I should have been brave, put myself out there, asked him if he wanted to try and figure something out rather than just burying my head in the sand as usual. Even if he'd said no, at least I wouldn't be left wondering. But what was done was done, I didn't have the time or energy to worry about it at that point in my life. Christmas with Daddy was only a few days away.

CHAPTER TWENTY THREE

—

Thursday 24th December

Cruising at seventy miles an hour with Radio One blaring out the Christmas tunes, I caught sight of myself in the rear view mirror, the girl that looking back at me even pastier than usual. I'd barely managed to scrape my hair up into a loose bun this morning and strands escaped wildly over my shoulders. I wore my comfiest skinny jeans, a pair of Ugg boots and a long ivory knitted jumper. The temperature on the dash board indicated that it was minus two outside, fitting I supposed for Christmas Eve.

The car was fit to burst with all my 'necessities',the boot may not have been enormous but the passenger seat managed to carry a whole pile of Christmas presents and other festive goodies.

Almost at Cairnryan, the port to board the boat to Ireland, I admired the views of the Scottish mountains, snow dusting the height of the peaks, leaving all thoughts of Edinburgh behind as I approached the ferry. It was two hours on the boat and I had another three hour's drive the other side of the water. I couldn't wait to be with my family, especially Daddy. It had been my absolute dream these past few weeks to be able to spend Christmas with him one more time.Albeit far from ideal, it was more than I could have dared to hope for, that first day we were reunited in the hospital.

My mind briefly flicked back to the image of Tom leaving the flat not even a week earlier and it felt like a life time ago. The gaping hole was still raw but I refused to look too deeply into it, although I was fully aware that we would be once again on the same stretch of land, albeit miles apart. I took a deep breath, popped an extra strong mint into my mouth and concentrated on the road ahead.

It was four thirty in the afternoon by the time I arrived in Galway City, the darkness was creeping in already and I was exhausted following the day of travelling. Jack waited for me in the car park next to his Golf, rubbing his hands together for warmth and I parked up into the space adjacent to him

'You look like you've squeezed half of Edinburgh into that little flashy hairdresser car of yours!' He engulfed me in one of his bear hugs.

'What are you doing waiting down here? Is Daddy ok?' I asked, terrified of coming so close to achieving my goal and falling at the last hurdle.

'He's fine. Just sleeping, more so than usual. It's taking its toll.' He looked serious all of a sudden. 'Orla... it won't be long now.'

My face sank visibly. Of course I'd known it all along but it didn't make it any easier. I'd deliberately not thought too far ahead, trying to take it one day at a time when my brain would allow it.

'I know Jack, of course. Let's just enjoy Christmas shall we? Stop pissing on my bonfire and have a look at what I've brought!' I couldn't face the seriousness of the situation so I reverted back to our Irish humour to make light from the grimness ahead of us.

Jack helped me pull out a Christmas wreath, an advent candle and a mountain of chocolate money which we used to love when we were kids. We made our way into the hospital together laden down with my accessories. The route was so familiar by then; up the stairs and to the end of the corridor, we passed by the nurses and greeted them warmly. They do such a fantastic job caring for the patients and don't get nearly enough credit for it. I'd been into many hospitals for various placements throughout my midwifery training and some of them had been absolutely awful, but not this one. The attitudes of the nurses were enviable. They were kind, compassionate and unbelievably discreet about the less dignified acts of care. They understood when to make small talk and when to leave well alone. I seriously admired them and so did Jack, but it helped that several of them were blonde with Australian accents, though that was another matter entirely.

'Hi Daddy.' We crept into his room quietly in case he was sleeping but he was just about awake.

'How are ya?' It was barely more than a whisper.

I handed him a glass of water which he was too weak to hold, his hands trembling. Holding it to his mouth for him I waited patiently for him to sip.

'Hardly a bloody Gin and Tonic, is it?' He feebly attempted to make light of the situation to cover his embarrassment over his increasing dependency. We laughed nevertheless. His head fell back heavily onto the pillow, every breath an effort, every movement an obvious chore.

'Look what I brought!' Deliberately ignoring his deterioration I pulled out the candle, the chocolate pennies and the wreath. The nurses had already put a tiny Christmas tree up on the windowsill.

'Like when you two were kids.' His eyes rolled and the lines crinkled further into his sunken ashen sockets, he looked shockingly close to death. I took his frail hand carefully, only realising now that as close as we were, he still might not make Christmas Day.

With the candle lit, Jack and I ate the chocolate money, merely for the sake of it. The sight of Daddy's deterioration in only a couple of days was enough to ensure it was difficult to stomach anything. We made small talk to remind him of our presence as he drifted in and out of consciousness. As the evening drew in his breathing laboured as he fought hard to stay with us.

'It's only one day, you know.' Jack whispered lightly. 'It's no different to any other day really.'

He was begging me to give Daddy permission to go, I know he was. My eyes welled with overflowing tears, running silently and heavy on my face. I nodded reluctantly, knowing at stage it wasn't fair for me to ask any more of him. He had battled long enough, the signs were on him as he twitched, uncomfortably troubled even in his unconscious state.

Two of Daddy's brothers arrived to sit with him. They offered to do the night shift for us and his sister Sheila was on her way as well. What they actually wanted was some time alone with him. I couldn't blame them but I was terrified to leave his side after I'd seen what had happened in the short few days that I'd been back in Edinburgh.

'Shall we go to Mammy's for a while?' Jack said, willing me to give our Uncles a chance to do what they needed to do.

'Can do I guess.' I was reluctant, terrified he wouldn't be here in the morning, but I understood the rest of the family needed time with him. My muscles were stiff as I rose from the plastic chair. Daddy stirred, eyes flickering briefly over me but he said nothing, slipping deeper away from us.

'Will he be ok?' I looked to Jack for reassurance. He nodded to one of the nurses, Natasha, at the desk only four feet outside Daddy's bedroom door.

'She will keep us updated.'

She nodded through the glass, sensing my need for assurance.

I kissed Daddy on the cheek and he murmured something unrecognizable under his breath. He didn't stir, the only noise was the regular beeping of the distribution of his life support. His brothers took our seats quietly next to him.

Mammy's house hadn't changed at all over the past twenty years, bar a fresh coat of beige paint. She was absolutely delighted to see us, welcoming us with hugs and kisses and her traditional Christmas sherry which we both detested, but we indulged her. It was impossible to feel festive, I checked my mobile phone again, fearful I would miss a call from the hospital, despite the fact I'd only just left.

I managed to tear myself away long enough to grab a quick shower, standing under the heat and steam trying to shake off the tension in my body. I changed into smarter jeans, brown boots and a red fitted jumper in an attempt to look more festive, even though I couldn't bring myself to feel it.

'Want to go to the local for a drink?' Jack asked. Another one of our Christmas traditions. It felt wrong in some ways but I wanted to carry on as normal for Breda as much as anything. There was nothing I could do for Daddy right now. His brothers and his sister would stay with him overnight. It wasn't just us he'd disappeared on all those years ago, it was everyone and each of them wanted to get their own time with him, understandably so. Jack had done last night on the arm chair in the hospital. I would do tomorrow night.

It had been ages since I'd seen anyone from home so I agreed. It stopped me from sitting staring at the clock, worrying if Daddy would actually make it to Christmas Day.

'Sure. Why not.' I pulled on my burgundy coat and woolly hat and we sauntered down the badly lit, narrow road to the local, McGinty's. We found two high bar stools and ordered two hot whiskeys with cloves and honey.

'I need something strong.' I said seriously. Was it terrible that I felt like a really good drink right now as our father lay in the hospital a few miles away, a hospital in which he would spend the remainder of what little time of his life he had left? Jack seemed to be on the exact same wave length as me as he gazed out the window although the only thing visible was our reflections.

'If Daddy were able, he would be sat at a bar right now too. I'm sure he really doesn't want us to be sat at his bedside moping twenty four seven. Besides I think we wear him out. And we both know very well how precious life is, so let's try and enjoy ourselves shall we? It is Christmas Eve after all.' He smiled at me encouragingly.

I honestly don't know what I would have done without him at that moment. He had been a Godsend. How people manage in these situations on their own is beyond me. We clinked our glasses together and make a toast.

'To Dad.' He says.

'To Daddy.' I agree.

The pub began to fill slowly with neighbours and friends that we barely ever crossed paths with except for on nights like this, Christmas Eve. The tinsel hung decoratively and the familiar carols that I had been intensely suffering for the last few weeks echoed in the background. There was no sign of Daragh Dunleavey tonight, he was probably at home with his family, which was the right place for him, waiting for Santa.

I briefly wondered where Tom was tonight. It was ironic how my original source of distraction was now the very thing I now needed distraction from. What would I do with both of the men I had loved, gone?

Mammy and Patrick landed in the pub after midnight mass, ordering a couple of glasses of red wine. Patrick rarely drank but it was Christmas after all. I took her hand, so glad to see her out. She was some woman for one woman, practically raising the two of us herself, in a time where divorce was actually illegal. She had done it all on her own, caring for us, providing for us, setting the strongest example she physically could.

'It's tradition, although I know things are different this year. We always usually join you for one.' She said, as though she needed to justify her appearance.

'I'm so glad you did Mam.' I squeezed her hand and she smiled warmly, waving at a few of the locals in the pub.

'How's your Daddy?' She asked.

'The same.' I replied, looking at her earnestly to see if she was ready to budge even a millimetre on her decision.

She nodded sombrely and changed the subject.

'I remember the days when you still believed in Santy, in fact you were convinced you saw him on the landing once. You must have been dreaming.' She smiled wistfully at the memory. Breda loved Christmas, a child herself at heart.

We ordered another round, the same again and I found Jack staring at me a bit too long.

'What?' I asked defensively.

'You're getting a bit skinny lady!' He said.

'Huh! I wish!' Although my jeans were hanging off me with the stress of everything.

'Whatever happened to that guy you were dating? Tom is it?' I knew he would bring it up at some point.

I paused to find the right words to tell him what happened, searching to see if I could talk about it without the emotion that I was trying so desperately to hide. I took a deep breath and composed myself and began.

'The thing is Jack I really liked him.' My lips were a little looser than I intended after the whiskey.

'So what happened?' He leaned in closer, arm on the bar, crouching lower to be at my eye level.

'He left. The audit finished, he's gone.'

'And did you not think about stopping him?' Jack asked.

'No. His life is in Dublin, mine is in Edinburgh.'

'Why would that stop you?'

I looked at him as though he were stupid but carried on.

'I tried to do long distance once before, don't you remember how that worked out?' I reminded him.

'That was ten years ago. You were children still. This is different.' He insisted.

'The timing doesn't help either. I can't think about anything else right now, it's not fair on Daddy. I want to give him as much of me as I possibly can, I can't be here, in Dublin and be working in Edinburgh.'

Jack dismissed my feeble explanation with a wave of his hand. 'Orla don't you think that it would be nice for Tom to meet Dad while he still could? That sounds like a poor excuse to me! Come on, I know you better than you realise. What's the real reason?'

'That is the real reason!'

'Ah I see.' He said almost smugly. 'You're afraid of getting hurt.'

'I am not!' I retorted a little too quickly.

'You are! That is the bottom line. You eventually met somebody, now you are actually frightened to pursue it in case you get hurt. Ha! I can't believe it. It's true isn't it?' He prodded me in the ribs. 'Don't be daft.' I flat out denied his accusation, but I had to acknowledge that he was right. I had been frightened, terrified in fact, unable to take firstly the rejection and secondly the thought of another long distance relationship.

'After Daragh you've spent years building a brick wall, block by block, carefully layered so as not to crumble, frightened of getting hurt again. Pick up the phone to him, little sis. Take some worldly advice from your big brother.' He paused again just for effect this time, almost smugly.

I rolled my eyes at my brothers so called 'worldly advice'.

I eyed him suspiciously, 'Why are you so interested in my love life all of a sudden anyway?'

He laughed and placed his arm around my shoulder loosely, 'I just don't want you to be an old spinster Midwife who has ten cats, stinks of piss and spends Saturday nights in knitting on her own in a creaky old wicker rocking chair!' It was the second time I'd heard that remark in the same amount of months.

We both laughed now and I punched him lightly on the arm, cheeky fecker.

'Seriously, I just want you to be happy. If you like this guy you should go for it. What have you got to lose?'

In my tipsy frame of mind he did make a good point. What have I got to lose? Then realised I had my pride, my dignity and worst of all, my heart.

'He left Edinburgh on Saturday and I haven't heard from him. Maybe it's for the best...' I said half-heartedly. I didn't add that the past week had felt like a year without him, that I'd checked my phone three thousand times only to be disappointed.

I didn't want to get hurt I admitted to myself, downing the rest of my drink. I also didn't want him to know about Daddy's illness, dragging him into my sorrows, for him to think he had to stay with me out of a sense of pity.

Jack seemed to sense my sombre mood and moved on to a lighter subject about which nurse he fancied from the hospital. Like father like son I suppose! I laughed along with him thoughts of Tom weighed heavily on my mind. Was I hiding behind my father's illness because I was scared? It felt was like opening a can of worms, pouring salt into an open wound. Did I cut my nose off to spite my face? I realised I was too proud to ask him if he'd like to try.

'Earth to Orla!' I tuned back in to find Jack waving another drink under my nose. The log fire next to us projected a wonderful cosy glow, the logs crackled and caused the light to flicker unpredictably. Breda and Patrick joined us once again, bidding the McMahon's a Merry Christmas.

'Sorry I was just thinking.' I said gazing into the fire at the burnt logs, some still on fire, some dead, some with fuel left in them. How appropriate to my state of mind.

'I think you should go for it sis.' He said quietly before Breda picked up on it.

'We'll see.' I whispered, mostly to myself.

CHAPTER TWENTY FOUR

—

25th December 2015

I awoke long before dawn in my childhood bedroom, with barely three hours of sleep. It was Christmas morning. I reached for my mobile phone on the locker next to me praying there was no change in the last eight hours, ringing the nurse's station directly. Daddy was in no position to answer his own phone anymore and I didn't want to disturb him.

'Oncology, Natasha here.' The blonde nurse who had started her night work before we left still had another hour of her shift to go.

'Natasha, it's Orla. How is he?' She was well used to my daily phone calls at this stage. It was reassuring to be able to pick up the phone at any hour of the day or night and get directly through to the women caring for him.

'No changes Orla. He stirred a few times in the night. Your family are still here.' She referred to my Uncles and Aunty.

'Thank you. I'll be in shortly. Merry Christmas.' I added as an afterthought.

I reached for the lamp that had been positioned next to my narrow single bed for the last twenty years, grasping the familiar outline until I found the switch and clicked it on. Westlife posters lined the wall secured with blue tack, I'd been a sucker for them at the time and I still wouldn't say no to Shane Filan even now.

Stretching my arms out above my head, I groggily rubbed the sleep out of my eyes. As I pulled back the covers the cold air in the room startled me. I needed to get to the hospital ASAP this morning and let Sheila go and get some sleep as well. Downstairs Mammy was already banging around preparing her usual Christmas feast, her two sisters and their husbands and children were coming over for the day. Everybody knew the situation with Daddy but for them, their lives continued on.

Mammy was burying her head in the sand and I worried that she'd regret it afterwards, but that was her business. She didn't want to see Daddy after everything and I got it. But he was threat at by that point. I wished she would just give him what he clearly needed, forgiveness and a goodbye.

I showered and dressed, pulling on a fitted, deep green jumper dress, black leggings and boots that extended just over my kneecap. I pulled my hair into a loose pony tail and pointlessly slapped on a bit of make-up. Jack was downstairs already holding three stockings bulging with gifts.

'Merry Christmas Sis.' He kissed me on the cheek, but there was a sobriety in his tone that didn't match his greeting.

'Merry Christmas.' I replied automatically, not feeling particularly merry, but grateful none the less that we had all got this far.

'Merry Christmas my darlings.' Breda enveloped us in an enormous hug then handed us a steaming hot mug of tea each. She perched on the edge of the old navy armchair, shifting uncomfortably on her bottom.

'Merry Christmas Mam.' I squeezed her hand, grateful for her understanding. None of it could have been easy on her either.

'How is he today?' She asked quietly.

'Barely conscious.' Jack replied before I could, not even attempting to hide the fact that in the last twelve hours Daddy hadn't woken properly, even once. The end was so close. I blinked back tears as I grabbed my coat and his, bypassing the ridiculous presents that I had foolishly bought for Daddy in the hope that he would hang on to open them. They taunted me now under the tree as I pulled on my hat and scarf. Even in my hurry I felt a contradictory sense of reluctance to go, tearing me in two. I thought 'This could be it today. I'm not ready, but would I ever be?'

'I've been wondering...' Mammy began.

I was in a desperate rush now, the end was imminent and I selfishly couldn't hang around to discuss the merits of what I knew she was going to say, it was too late for discussion, she would have to decide herself at this stage.

'Mammy, either way, it's ok. Do what's right for you.' I placed Jack's car keys in his hand having located them by the front door and practically pushed him out into the cold, frosty morning. It felt as though it could snow at any minute, enormous heavy white clouds loomed overhead.Breda flung a tea towel over her shoulder and waved us off with a tight lipped smile that didn't quite reach her eyes.

The hospital itself was no different to yesterday but the atmosphere felt different, it was Christmas Day after all. We passed some of the same patients that we regularly met on the way up to Daddy, smiling and exchanging festive greetings to those that were well enough to notice us racing through. However sad it was to see the really sick patients with their families sitting lovingly around them, painting on a brave face, it was so much worse to see the ones with no families around them, merely tubes and machinery to keep them company at Christmas.

We reached Daddy's room, surging in this time, once again feeling fortunate to be able to spend the day together with him still here.

I skidded to an abrupt halt with Jack flying hard into the back of me as I saw the bed was empty. My heart sank. I squeezed my eyes tightly and reopened them hoping I'd imagined it. No, the bed was still empty. 'Oh God please don't let it be now, not today of all days.' I pleaded in my mind. I stood rigid, a rabbit caught in the headlights but then I heard a voice in the corner of the room behind the door.

'I'm over here don't panic.' He uttered, barely a croak of a whisper.

'Dad you scared the absolute shit out of us!' Jack exclaimed.

I took it all in as I waited for my heart rate to return to normal. Daddy was propped up with a stack of pillows in the old armchair in the corner, tubes still in place but the unit had been moved. He must have been carried over, there was absolutely no way he could have made it by himself, he hadn't left the bed in almost two weeks. In fact he had barely been conscious at all in the last twenty four hours.

This was my fault for putting all my foolish emphasis on one stupid day. Propped up like that his condition was visibly exposed, frailer than ever before, his arms were thinner than my own. It expended an awful amount of his energy to merely sit up like that. They sometimes say that terminally ill patients sometimes get a rush, a last lease of life before they go, before they leave this world for good, and I wondered I that was what was happening now.

'I wanted to sit up with you… I wanted to…' He couldn't continue, weak, his heavy head sank back onto the pillow propped behind him, his voice rasping. He coughed, spluttering tiny flecks of blood from his diseased lungs. The spirit of our old proud Dad was crystal clear, even in the sunken shape of the sickly man in front of me.

'Daddy back to bed please, just be comfortable.'

Jack called the nurses and three of them put Dad back to bed as his eyes rolled back in his head, the exhaustion all too much. He was unconscious again within seconds.

'What did you let him do that for?' Jack asked the nurse who had clearly taken over only an hour ago.

'I had no choice, stubborn git started trying to pull tubes out of himself if I didn't do what he asked, I'm not having him popping it on my watch, especially today of all days.' She diffused the situation expertly and we even managed a small snigger, knowing all too well what a stubborn bastard he could be when the fancy took him.

'Look at what Santa left under the tree for you!' Jack held up one of the stockings I didn't realise he had brought in with him. I examined it closer and noted it actually had 'Orla' stitched on the side in white. Jack surprised me with his thoughtfulness, then I realised it had Mammy's handiwork stamped all over it.

I stuck my hand into the deepest part of the scratchy mesh stocking and fished out a bottle of Coco Chanel and a framed photo of Dad aged about twenty five with a fag hanging out of the side of his mouth and a clear twinkle in his eye. It was a beautiful picture, one I'd never seen before. Breda must have been up in the attic. I also came across the compulsory tangerine and a euro coin, a life-long tradition in our house.

Jack opened his to find a bottle of Armani Code, a framed photo cut out from a lads mag of Kelly Brook, and the mandatory tangerine and euro coin. Breda cracked us up and I wondered again if she would come. I pictured her bustling around the kitchen with her sisters fussing over their husbands, entertaining in a way that she couldn't help but love. But I knew her heart wasn't in it, I'd seen her wavering this morning. Whatever had happened in the past, however awful it was, was best left there. Her faith was strong, she believed in forgiveness. I felt it in my heart that she would come.

The hours ticked by with no change, a doctor called in late in the morning to check Daddy's observations. As he acknowledged the shallow rate of breathing, he looked at us intently, to confirm our understanding of the situation. We were both gravely aware. Along the corridor the forced merriment of some of the other patients could clearly be heard. The inmates, as Dad has described them all only a few short weeks ago, himself included. Forced to portray an upbeat persona all because of the day it was, families perched around clean, starched hospital beds, as if it were the most natural thing in the world, attempting to behave as though this was the only place to be on Christmas Day. God love them all. There was only silence by Daddy's bedside, bar the beeping of the monitors and that strained rattle for breath, a sound that would haunt me forever.

Jack quietly stared into space. Intermittently one of us would get a burst of energy and try and strike up a conversation, but mostly we remained silent with heavy hearts.

Another of Dads sisters, Julie and his brother, Johnny arrived in the early afternoon. It was a relief to see them, it had been years really since I'd seen any of them. We'd drifted apart over the years as families do, especially given the broken circumstances of our own home. They jollied up the atmosphere for a short while and it was a welcome distraction from the impending fate of my father.

Sitting with us for a couple of hours, they brought turkey sandwiches on plate and delicious looking ham with homemade soda bread. I forced myself to eat for sustenance, though I tasted absolutely nothing. They left then, better for having seen Daddy, although he appeared not to have noticed their arrival, or departure either. He was slowly slipping away from me as each hour passed. The sun set on Christmas Day, snowflakes gently tapped on the hospital window. The day that I had begged him to hang on for had almost passed. A round heavy tear rolled helplessly down the length of my cheek and dropped onto my leggings below. I took his hand gently and squeezed it, with no response, not even a twitch. The rattle continued to echo mercilessly throughout the room as he struggled on.

CHAPTER TWENTY FIVE

—

Monday 28ᵗʰ December

In the days that passed we spent almost every waking moment there, bar the odd few hours to go back to Breda's to shower and change, taking it in turns, one of us with him constantly. I sat to the right side of Daddy, perched on the edge of the hospital bed and Jack sat to the left. Both of us clutched at lukewarm cups of tea, just for something to do with our hands. The support machine let out an irregular beep now and again, breaking the silence of the hospital room as it regulated oxygen levels and dispensed more morphine. It was late. Or maybe it was very early. The hospital was the quietest I'd ever known it, the earlier visitors had all left the building in search of the comfort of their own homes.

The nurse said it would only be a matter of hours now, but that was seventeen hours ago. He hadn't stirred or moved a muscle in that entire time. Jack and I both tried talking to him, desperate for him to know we were there with him, that we would be there with him until the end. I was slowly beginning to accept that this was it.

But Daddy was still fighting on and although it was shallow and ragged, he continues to draw breath, refusing to give, though we knew it was imminent. The nurses regularly but discreetly entered the room, monitoring the situation, so accustomed to dealing with this every day. I don't know how they do it.

A slow trickle of blood began to run from Daddy's nose. I gently wiped it away with a tissue from the side of the bed. His insides were giving up and shutting down. Taking his hand carefully, I squeezed it ever so slightly. No response again, nothing at all

'I wonder what he's waiting for?' I voiced my thoughts aloud in a hushed whisper.

In a moment of acute realisation I accidently hit the nail on the head.He was waiting for something, he had to be. We were both here, we had been lucky enough not only to make our peace but to get to know each other again.

I glanced swiftly up at Jack, suddenly undeniably sure.

Jack's head snapped round to look straight at me and I knew he knew what I was thinking. More to the point, he knew I was right, I could see it in his eyes.

'Mammy.' We both whispered at the same time.

The quiet vibration of my phone startled me. I squinted down at the screen to check the caller identity, not a bit surprised to see that it was her. As a family, the three of us had always been close, almost frighteningly so. Despite the fact we all lived apart, our intuitive bond was irrevocably strong.

'Mam?' I answered in a low voice.

'How is he darling?' She asked anxiously.

'Just the same...' I paused, looking at Jack for inspiration.

'Orla,' She hesitated uncertainly, 'You might think this sounds super crazy and maybe even possibly a little bit vain of me but... it did occur to me... I mean...' She battled to get the words out right. Unbelievable how our tiny family unit seemed to be supernaturally subconsciously connected at this momentous time.

'Do you think he's waiting for me?' Her voice broke, heavy with emotion as she said the words I silently prayed for.

'Yes, Mammy. I didn't want to say it, to pressure you, if you didn't want to, but yes. I think he is.It literally just this second occurred to me, then you rang.'

'I'm on my way.' She hung up before I could even say I love her.

'She's coming.' I told Daddy and stroked his hand gently.

The regular ticking of the clock on the wall seemed loud, out of place in the quiet of the hospital. We watched the minutes pass by and then an hour. The sun eventually rose, feeble weak winter rays shone through the glass of the window, melting the tiny remaining traces of snow from the panes. It reminded me of that morning many moons ago when I woke up to The Letter.

The unmistakable clicking of heels approached from along the corridor, closer and closer, then stopped abruptly outside Daddy's door. The handle turned slowly, her silhouette visible through the glass square of the opening door and she inched in cautiously. Breda's head appeared first, entering the room her eyes rested sadly on our father, once her husband, as she took him in. She held a scarf and gloves in her trembling hands. The bags around her eyes indicated that she had been awake as long as we had. I greet her warmly with a relieved embrace in turn and she edged closer to the bed.

'Hello Michael.' She said lowly, using his full Christian name. She shook her head in obvious sorrow, shocked at his helpless condition, her first husband, the love of her life. The bane of her life.

'How did you get here?' Jack asked, pulling up another chair on his side of the bed.

'Patrick drove me. He insisted.' She answered, a million miles away, deep in thought.

'Do you want a minute on your own?' I asked discreetly.

'Would you mind love?' She looked from me to Jack, then back to me again.

'Of course not.' We both agreed, tiptoeing out of the room to give them some peace. I touched Dad's hand as I passed towards the door and still he did not even flicker an eyelid. His pillows were propped up high, his head turned to the left, the same position he'd been in for hours. I shut the door carefully behind us to give Breda some privacy.

We headed for the toilets and then the canteen. Neither of us could bear to eat a thing but we opted for the terrible tea again just for something to do. We sat silently, no words to comfort each other at that stage. Waiting, wondering, willing, as awful as it sounded. I felt sick to my stomach with the anticipation of the inevitable and strangely empty.

After almost an hour we made our way back to the room. My body was loudly protesting against coordination, stumbling into the wall of the corridor. I was shattered but I couldn't afford to close my eyes for even a minute, frightened he would go if I fell asleep. Jack knocked lightly before opening the door to let Breda know we were back.

'Hi kids.' Her face was covered in red raw blotches from crying.

Daddy hadn't moved an inch.

'He's just the same.' She informed us, dabbing her eye with a crinkled tissue from her jeans pocket.

'I spilled my guts to him and he didn't even bat an eyelash. I hope he knows we are all here now. I hope he can hear us.' She wiped a stray tear from the corner of her eye.

'Where is Patrick now Mum?' I asked.

'He's reading the paper in the car, he thought we might just want to be us, like before. He said to fetch him if we need him.'

The nurse came in again and brought more tea and sugary biscuits, probably to help keep us awake. I ate two custard creams and tasted nothing. The three of us sat around my father's bed talking softly about everything and nothing. Jack told Mam about a case he was working on, I told her that Samantha had asked me to be her bridesmaid in June. It was so surreal. After a while we fell quiet again, each sinking back into our own thoughts. Jack looked like I felt; exhausted and he slumped forward resting his head in his hands.

Breda broke the silence, never taking her eyes off my father and she began to speak with a raw emotion that took me aback. She'd previously sheltered us from any of her emotions towards our father, protected us from the awful details of what really happened back in the day.

'I just wonder what he thought of me after everything.... everything that happened...all that we went through. I wonder if he looked at you two and thought I did a good job.... I'll never know if he had the same regrets that I do.... Most of all I wonder if he ever really loved me....' Her voice splintered with uncontrollable emotion.

I began to see my Mother as a young lady, impressionable, vulnerable, wanting to be loved by the man that she had married so young. She had adored him in her day. We all knew that. She had held him on a pedestal, even when he left she'd been heard to say she couldn't live with him, she didn't even like him, but my God how she had loved him.

'Look!' Jack nodded towards the bed, straightening himself to get a closer look.

Daddy's eyes flickered ever so slightly, a low, gruff, incomprehensible noise escaping from the guttural depths of his throat. His frail fingers slid out slowly as he fumbled with the side of the starchy sheet. His curious eyes opened, squinting slits at first, gradually adjusting to the wintery light streaming in through the steamy window. He attempted to reach out for Breda, as weak as he was, not taking his eyes from her startled face.

She took his hand and they looked at each other intently, silent seconds passing by marked only by the intrusive ticking of the wall clock, the only other sound being Daddy's ragged fight for breath. The determined glint in his eyes highlighted the emotion he felt for her, leaving her in absolutely no doubt of the intensity of the love he had for her, the heartfelt sorrow, the regret and the pain. She took his hand as they locked eyes for the very last time. With Jack and I sat on the other side of the bed, he closed his eyes peacefully and gently slipped away from us.

The fact that it was so emotional, even beautiful at the end, if that were even possible, masked the underlying desperation and devastation I harboured, for a short time at least. He was waiting for her. The entire act of him opening his eyes in response to Breda's questions, the silent but deeply significant exchange between them lasting less than thirty seconds but feeling like so much more. Then he was gone.

He gave her what she needed to know to go on with her life and she in return gave him what he needed to leave this earth in peace.

It was by far the most bizarre but beautiful scene I had witnessed or been part of in my twenty eight years. If he had to go, then it was the best possible goodbye for all of us. In many ways we were lucky. Lucky that we had been there, grateful that we got to say goodbye and thankful that we had time to prepare, not that you could ever be prepared for what happened in there.

Jack and Mammy stayed with my father's body for a while after the Doctor had been in to certify his death. I couldn't. The room felt stifling all of a sudden and besides, there was no point, my Daddy was gone.

Oddly, I'd expected to see something at the moment of his death. For years it had been instilled in us by the Catholic Church that our souls would go to heaven when we passed and stupidly I had expected to see something. It was the first adult I'd witnessed pass. Sadly I'd seen several babies go in my time and that was something that would stay with me forever, but it had been different, I'd been at work. This was so personal to me.

'I'm going to get some air.' I told them, leaving the room, taking a lingering look at my father's empty body for the last time before the undertaker arrived. I kissed him on the forehead one final time. The tears fell freely, it was a relief to him in the end, he had suffered enough, fought so hard to stay with us for as long as he could.

I nodded at the girls as I passed the nurse's station, they acknowledged me sympathetically as I continued down the corridor. I stepped into the lift alone.

Strangely, I didn't feel alone. I'm not a believer in ghosts, or anything overly spiritual at all. Despite my Catholic upbringing I've never been one for wondering about the afterlife, far too preoccupied in my current life. I'm a cynic. I regularly say out loud that if there is anything out there, I for one do not wish to know about it. It would freak the shite out of me. Maybe that was why I'd seen nothing at the final minute.

Yet in that precise moment in time, an undeniably warm glow surrounded me, enveloping me, akin to the heat of another body occupying the tiny space with me. I felt a presence so strongly, that until that moment I would never have believed it to be possible. My Father's strength was with me in spirit, I was certain that was what it was, undeniably in my heart of hearts, part of him was there with me still.

Stepping out of the lift I made my way through the automatic doors to the outside of the hospital building for the long craved fresh air, pausing for a split second to check that the feeling was still with me. Again I felt the warmth surrounding me, despite the bitter cold December air. It was oddly reassuring.

I found myself walking towards a nearby bench, on a small piece of grass overlooking the parking lot. I allowed myself to be guided by the warmth, it led me, pulling me certainly to sit down on the frost dusted wooden bench. I closed my eyes, basking in the warmth next to me. The winter sunlight illuminated my face and I was desperate to hang on to the feeling, I didn't want his spirit to leave me. With my eyes still closed I tilted my cheeks up to the warmth and embraced the moment, hoping the feeling would stay with me forever. I felt reassured and in a strange way, oddly complete, so sure I was not alone, aware only of the warmth and the peace that I felt inside.

As suddenly as it came, the feeling began to slowly evaporate, leaving me once again. I desperately tried to cling on to it, every fibre of my being willing it to stay, but it was no good, it faded gradually until it remained only in my heart. But by that point I knew then that I would never be completely alone. I'd carry that feeling with me from then on, drawing strength from it in future times of need.

I sat quietly with my eyes closed storing every single memory, every detail of the experience, the warmth safely inside my head and my heart, desperate to capture it all while it was fresh with me, that feeling of strength and certainty.

After a short while a shadow hovered in front of me, obstructing my light, blocking the sun from my face. I was so very tired, it had been a long seventy eight hours.

I opened my eyes to check what the enormous obstruction stealing my sunshine was.

'Tom?' I was startled to see him, beautiful and surprised in front of me. For a split second I wondered if I had nodded off in my sleep deprived state and I blinked hard twice to check.

'Orla! What the hell are you doing here?' He gawped at me from head to toe, digesting the two day old crumpled clothing and scraped back greasy hair, my face tear stained with mascara. My cheeks were wet to my hand, I hadn't realised that I was still silently crying. Tears of relief, guilt and fatigue.

He reached for me, I could barely stand but he held me up, supporting me, squeezing me fiercely into his strong familiar arms. He kissed my tear stained cheeks before kissing me lightly on the lips, uncertainly.

I responded to him the way I had done so many times before, my body still attracted to his so physically, despite the circumstances, he pulled me like a magnetic force. I kissed him fully, savouring his lips on mine for a few seconds until everything flooded back and I broke away.

'Tom. What are you doing here? How did you know I was here?' I couldn't believe he was actually standing in front of me, so smart, so familiar in his suit and tie. Smart but cold.

'Where's your coat?' I asked him stupidly, probably in shock.

'Orla, what do you mean how did I know you were here? I didn't know you were here!' He ignored the insignificant matter of his current attire.

'If you didn't know I was here then what are you doing here?' I was really confused now.

'I work here Orla! I'm auditing this hospital.'

'Auditing the hospital. Of course.' I repeated like a dazed parrot. I'd forgot it was a normal working day for the rest of the world, Christmas had passed, New Year still yet to come.

'Are you okay? You don't look so good.' He looked at me with concern radiating from his big blue eyes.He held onto me, almost afraid to let go.

'I'm okay... I think... Daddy, he's here. He was here...' I tried to explain but the words didn't want to come.

Understanding flooded between us and I could see Tom piecing the bits together, memories of our time together, my frequent family phone calls and trips away and vague reference to Daddy being sick all falling into place for him.

'It's okay...Sh.' He hushed me soothingly, stroking my hair, holding me to his strong supple chest. But I didn't want to be shushed, I wanted to tell him more. There'd been something I'd been wanting to tell him for a while. I couldn't quite bring myself to say it before, always afraid, always hiding behind the armour I didn't fully realise I wielded until Jack had so kindly pointed it out on Christmas Eve.

After the events of the previous few days, not to mention the weeks before hand, I'd come to appreciate the fragility of life. The preciousness of each and every single one of the tiny moments that make up all of our own stories. Instead of my new awareness terrifying me, invoking a vulnerability in me, the loss of my father drove me to embrace it, embrace life, the fear of getting hurt included.

'I love you.' The words tumbled awkwardly from my lips. The words I was so afraid of, the feelings I'd been hiding from, terrified to admit that I needed him, petrified of his rejection.

'I love you too Orla, from the moment I laid eyes on you in that bar in Edinburgh. You don't make it easy to get close to you though girl, I wanted to tell you I'd be here, but you didn't want to know. Now I know why.' He looked sincerely into my eyes and we clung to each other tightly. I was unable to let go of him even for a moment.

As the sun beamed down on us outside the hospital, I felt this was Daddy's doing, so sure he had led me there to that very bench deliberately. The warmth was back, but it was a different kind, one that was there to stay, I was sure of it. Surer than I'd ever been about anything.

'I suppose I should take you up to meet my family then?' I nodded up to the hospital windows high above and I swore I could see Jack and Breda squinting down at us.

'I suppose you should.' He replied, his strong hand taking mine firmly, leading me back into the building. I'd left with one man and returned with another.

CHAPTER TWENTY SIX

—

Tuesday 28th December 2015

The girls arrived in Galway for the funeral to be by my side. It was so good of them to travel all that way for me. Rebecca rang the doorbell of Mammy's Georgian house, she'd been there several times before over the years.

'I'm so sorry for your loss.' She handed me a beautiful bouquet of lilies and threw her arms around me tightly. I had to turn away, my eyes welling up with emotion again. Doing a double take over her shoulder, I noticed a man standing at the foot of our drive way. Rebecca waved him up to us.

'I brought someone, I hope you don't mind.' Rebecca looked momentarily awkward.

I laughed out loud in utter surprise as the penny finally dropped.

Samantha's school friend Daniel approached us and shook my hand in condolence before placing his arm loosely around Rebecca.

'I can't believe it!' I said in shock, hugging them both. Why she couldn't tell us before was beyond me.

'I didn't want to jinx it.' She shrugged.

'Does Samantha know?' I asked, just as Samantha and Simon pulled into the driveway in a hire car from Dublin.

'I rang her earlier. She was over the moon.' Rebecca smiled, relieved her secret was out in the open once and for all.

Despite my own sorrow about Daddy I was so delighted that everything was working out for my two best friends and for me as well seemingly.

Daddy's untimely departure was a given since that very letter. The fact that Tom was there with me was something I would be forever grateful to both of them for, however it had happened, whatever led us both to be there outside that hospital.

'I'm so sorry sweetheart.' Samantha put her arms around me and again I fought the tears that threatened to shed with the kindness of my friends. Our guests entered the hallway that hosted the encounter that had led to me to meet them all in the first place, so many years ago.

Rebecca greeted Breda and Jack, offering condolences and she introduced Daniel to them. Breda fussed around everybody, fetching drinks and handing round plates of sandwiches.

'To Daddy.' I raised my glass and toasted him, clinking glasses with my nearest friends and family, grateful to have gained so much, even through our loss.

CHAPTER TWENTY SEVEN

—

Wednesday 30th December

The funeral was arranged immediately after Daddy's passing. Things were done very quickly in Ireland. The tiredness eventually caught up with me, travelling most weeks had been so physically exhausting, not to mention emotionally draining, though I wouldn't have swapped it for the world.

The girls had been a great source of support, ordering flowers and making arrangements for the wake. Jack had been an absolute rock. Daddy didn't make a will, so we had no idea what he wanted us to do. We'd never thought to ask throughout the course of the time we had spent together, it would have been all too real and raw to have brought it up. My brother bravely made the big decisions and decided to go with a cremation, then to bury Dad's ashes in his family plot alongside his own parents and baby brother. It was unusual to have a cremation in the West of Ireland but Jack was adamant it was the right thing to do.

Tom was still working at the hospital on his audit. It was strange to think of him working in the place that I had come to know so well, that had come to mean so much to me. The hours we spent there would stay with me forever emblazoned on my heart. The warm glow remained with me and I was so sure that Tom and I were brought back together deliberately.

I regularly caught myself talking out loud to Daddy in the hope that he could hear me. With all that had happened it really left me pondering about the greater meaning of life and where people go when they pass. Being brought up in a Catholic country, I expected to almost see Daddy go up to heaven, as daft as it sounds. Where did he go? I'm sure wherever he is, he's at peace. Most of the time I didn't feel sad. I felt very grateful.

Friday morning dawned with crisp sunshine reflecting off a thin layer of snow on the ground, at least the day was bright. I felt sure it was a sign, the sunshine. The last time it shone on my face like that was when my father left us and when Tom came back into my life and in some ways it stayed with me, in me, since.

We arrived at the church early to greet the people attending. I had no idea if many would attend to pay their respects or not, it dawned on me how little I knew about Daddy's life over the past twenty years. During the time we spent together he always wanted to know the things that I'd been doing, it had only just struck me that he never actually talked about what he had been doing for all those absent years.

In the church archway I stood with Jack to my left and Breda to my right, Samantha close behind us with Simon, Tom, Rebecca and Daniel. Head to toe in black, I managed to find a smart suit and fitted blouse, covered with the warmest coat I could find, black leather gloves grasped tightly in my hands at the ready.

Around my neck I wore my father's wedding band on a necklace that Jack had given to me. I ran my fingers over it lightly fingering the metal. It was the only personal belonging of his that I owned and it meant the world to me.

The number of people pouring into the church caught me by surprise; friends, neighbours, colleagues all shook hands and offered condolences, many of whom Breda knew from back in the day. Some of whom none of us knew. Uncles, Aunts, Cousin's; all united in support. Irish funerals are as big as Irish weddings. Even the nurses from the hospital arrived to pay their respects. I even caught a glimpse of Keira Callen, my childhood friend from many moons ago.

Jack and I sat in the front row of the packed Church, arms linked in solidarity. It was as cold inside as it was outside, the stained glass windows doing nothing for the insulation. Untraditionally the closed coffin rested on the altar at the front. Daddy wouldn't have wanted to be remembered at his weakest. Instead a photo of his earlier days rested in a frame on top of the polished wood bearing flowers consisting of letters spelling out DADDY.

The priest began the service and we bowed our heads respectfully. Through the sorrow I was so deeply grateful, feeling Daddy leading me to Tom was a parting gift. A constant reminder that I would never be alone.

We said The Lord's Prayer and Father Andrews talked about my father, briefly outlining his life, his children, his family and friends. Daddy fancied himself to be a bit of a country singer back in his day and could usually be found in the local pub singing folksongs. We smiled in remembrance of happier times.

My brother bravely stood to say a few words about our Dad and he did so very well. Struggling with emotion in parts, he delivered a short but powerful speech before carrying the coffin alongside Patrick, Tom and Daddy's brothers.

The organist played a hymn, I took a huge breath as the boys transported the coffin away to the sleek black car. It broke my heart to think that Daddy was actually in there and I would never see him again. The tears rolled down my cheeks uncontrollably and Breda and I clung on to each other for dear life while Tom watched on, silently strong.

Dinner and drinks were arranged at my father's local pub afterwards and we made our way there in several cars. Breda went with Patrick and Jack and I went with Tom and Samantha. Meeting people that knew Daddy in the years we were all estranged brought me a different kind of comfort. I even found myself laughing, something I had not anticipated for my father's funeral. I was comforted to hear that he always talked of us proudly. Listening to stories from his colleagues of drunken debauchery and fun made me smile, still getting to know him further even if it was through second hand experiences. Tom hovered close and I was visibly stronger in the knowledge he was there.

I spotted Jack at a table with the nurses. Nudging Breda to look over, we both agreed that Jack was a chip off the old block.

'If Daddy were still here he'd be sat with the pretty blonde nurses too.' I stated.

She agreed, smiling wryly at me, knowing all too well it was God's honest truth.

People began to slip away throughout the afternoon and evening, duty done, condolences expressed. I was left with my nearest and dearest; Breda, Patrick, Jack, Samantha, Rebecca and Tom. It had been a long couple of days and the exhaustion crept in.Breda and Patrick left first, desperate to shut the door on the world for the night and put their feet up in front of the fire to reflect on everything. Mammy hugged me tightly and whispered, 'I am so proud of you girl and your Daddy is too.'

Samantha and Simon left next to get the overnight boat as they were both working in the hospital the following night. I made her promise to text me when she got home and thanked her for her support.

Jack stood next to announce he was meeting an old friend for a drink. If you believed that you'd believe anything, my money was on the blonde nurse with the long hair and doe eyes and I told him so. He brushed it off with a smirk.

That just left Tom and I sat in my father's local with a glass of wine and each other for company. I tried to picture Daddy here, imagined him propping up the bar with his whiskey chasers, chancing his arm with some of his not so smooth one liners to the barmaid. It was an oddly comforting thought.

'Shall we go?' I asked Tom, finishing my drink.

'Whenever you're ready sweetheart.' He replied.

We left the pub and made our way back to his hotel accommodation provided for the duration of this part of the audit. As we strolled hand in hand down the narrow streets of red brick, terraced houses, I began to appreciate how much I'd changed over the last ten days.

I looked forward to the New Year, a new start, liberatingly no longer scared of commitment, determined to make the most of every day this unpredictable life allowed me, destined to spend every minute of the days that God gives me with the wonderful man on my right. He squeezed my hand knowingly, glancing down with a reassuring smile and it was an unspoken agreement between us. It looked like I could be coming home....

EPILOGUE

Two Years Later

My eyes darted around the brightly lit room taking in the familiar equipment, the monitors, pain relief, gloves and charts. I looked at drawer upon drawer of packs of sterile instruments that I prayed to God I would not need. Sweat beaded my forehead, my spine felt like it was about to snap in two and all of my dignity had gone out of the window hours ago.

At least in this hospital I knew nobody. Since I moved to Dublin over a year ago I'd managed to secure a Community Midwife position in a lovely little practice in Dun Laoghaire. This was the first time I'd seen the inside of a Labour Ward in a long time. As the epic pain engulfed me, I vowed I wouldn't be rushing back to see it again anytime soon either.

I was close, I knew it myself. Not much longer and we would lay our eyes and hands on our baby, half of him and half of me, our own little miracle. It was this unquestionable fact that spurred me on, forcing me to draw strength that I wasn't aware I owned. Gritting my teeth I bore the agony as quietly as I could, mortified to be the midwife screaming for the epidural, yet it was on the tip of my tongue and reflected in the whites of my clenched, tense knuckles.

The midwife in charge of us watched on, quietly encouraging me. She leaned down and examined parts of me that I had never seen on myself.

'You're ready.' She nodded encouragingly.

I began to push. Tom stood next to the bed holding my right leg up, supporting the entire weight of it as I writhed and wriggled on my side, doubled over with the overwhelming excruciating pressure of the next contraction.

'You're doing so well honey, you're a powerhouse.' He was my everything, my light and my life. His constant unwavering support drove me to push on, anxiety apparent in his tired eyes as he waited anxiously for this part to all to be over, so close to meeting the other love of his life.

Eight minutes later a piercing cry echoed around the tiny yellow room and I looked down to lay my eyes on our beautiful baby boy, the most gorgeous creature I had ever seen in my entire thirty years. Tears of sweet joy and relief streamed from my face as I laughed and cried in delight at our precious, healthy bundle placed on my bare chest. The overwhelming rush of love I harboured for this tiny delicate child was unparalleled to anything I'd ever experienced before.

Tom put his arms around both of us tightly, nuzzling in gently to smell our son, to feel his soft, sticky, innocent skin. He kissed me firmly on the mouth and looked at me with a new found respect that could only be attributed to witnessing the birth of your own flesh and blood. Similarly to me all those years ago, he had now seen a real life superhero in the flesh, crystal clear enlightenment clearly displayed in the unshed tears in his eyes.

'Michael.' I said, glancing from my baby to my husband, questioningly.

'Michael Thomas Rourke.' Tom suggested and I agreed whole heartedly, a combination of both the men I loved in my life.

The warmth enveloped me, surrounding me. In that moment, I was sure he was watching over us. I was complete.

Lyndsey Gallagher is a Dental Hygienist by day and a fictional Author by night. She lives in the West of Ireland with her husband and their two toddlers. An avid reader herself, she hosts a radio Book Club called 'All Booked Up' on www.bcrfm.ie tune in on Sundays to listen in.

Other titles by Lyndsey Gallagher-
The Seven Year Itch (May 2019)
How Will I Know? (February 2020)

Subscribe to Lyndsey's mailing list for future updates and new releases at www.lyndseygallagherauthor.comIG @ lyndseygallagherauthor

Printed in Great Britain
by Amazon

55317439R00130